POSTMARK CHRISTMAS

POSTMARK CHRISTMAS

A Holiday Romance Novel

KATIE BACHAND

MINNEAPOLIS, MN

ISBN 978-1-7334326-4-1

FIRST EDITION

Cover Illustration and Design by Lance Buckley Design
Book Design by KB
Author Image by Studio Twelve:52

BOOKS BY KATIE BACHAND

SERIES

Taking Chances Series:
Becoming Us (Prequel)
Conflict of Interest (#1)
In the Business of Love (#2)
A Business Affair (#3)
Betting on Us (#4)

STANDALONES

Romantic Comedy:
The Problem with Love Potions

Christmas Novels:
Postmark Christmas
Waiting on Christmas
A Borrowed Christmas Love Story
The Worst Christmas Wife

JOIN KATIE'S NEWSLETTER

Head to Katie's website at
www.katiebachandauthor.com
and join her newsletter for fun content, great deals, free books,
and more.

Or, simply scan the QR code below.
(Hover your phone camera over the image!)

Enjoy!

For Lisa,
And all of the amazing holidays
We were able to spend together.

POSTMARK CHRISTMAS

CHAPTER 1

Harlow Hill had been listening to Christmas music since July. She told herself it was because of the job. Her clients started putting together holiday commercials, print advertisements, and plans for their festive – and usually over-the-top – holiday parties even before their Independence Day events were over.

But she knew, even without the big-ticket clients and events, she would still be yearning for Christmas. She would be sneaking in a holiday music session while working out, or turning the air conditioning up at The Hill – her inherited Victorian mansion on Summit Avenue – and throwing on some cozy winter pajamas, opening a bottle of eggnog, and settling in for the Hallmark Channel's *Christmas in July* event.

Thank God somebody out there had the right mind to air adorable, romantic Christmas movies when the temperature outside was ninety-eight and the air so humid your glasses would fog up just moving from inside to out.

Sally, who was preparing to give her weekly project update, was just as excited about it as Harlow. Though she was usually a little less restrained and reserved in her presentation.

"Hi! Good morning! Are you ready for our update?" Sally asked as she bounded into Harlow's office, her words a mixture of singing and shouting.

Sally, Harlow noted upon her entrance, was wearing the same winter white color of the walls and the same red accent. Only instead of concrete, her sweater was a chunky knit, and instead of red picture frames and vases, her earrings and necklace were a mixture of berry-red beads and feathers.

Harlow couldn't help but smile at the enthusiastic young woman. Sally wasn't unlike Harlow had been as a young marketing and advertising executive. Maybe that's why she'd always had a soft spot for the vibrant, and ambitious brunette.

"I am absolutely ready. Come in. Who else is joining today?" Harlow gestured to the leather chesterfield sofa across from her desk, and Sally sat.

Harlow knew Sally wouldn't need any of the staff to help in the breakdown of every excruciating and finite detail of their plans, but Sally – and Harlow too, admittedly – loved having the room filled and hearing from the team as they recounted the status of the projects they owned. All of them were competitive, but overwhelmingly supportive.

"We'll have Ryan and Vanessa. Jacquelyn is on-site setting up for her skating event this weekend. Which, if I might add, is amazing." Sally said, while her hazel eyes grew two sizes, letting a dreamy haze cloud across them as she looked off into the distance. "Her decision to go with *A Log Cabin Christmas theme* was dead-on. The evergreens she brought in are the perfect pine green, and they are adorned with these chunky amber lights, fragrant cinnamon pinecones, red robin ornaments, and the presents are wrapped in buffalo-check paper. Seriously, it's like walking into an LL Bean catalog."

"Oh my God, are you talking about *A Log Cabin Christmas?*" Vanessa asked, catching the last couple words while running through the door. Attempting to be on time once this week, and to not spill her coffee upon entry. "It is glorious and rugged perfection. It makes me want to live in a cabin and dress in plaid."

Vanessa plopped next to Sally on the chesterfield as Ryan sauntered in, completely cool and unfazed that he was five minutes late. He took one of the wooden chairs that bordered the couch, sliding effortlessly in and offering a killer smile.

Oh the hearts he would break, Harlow thought, and the pining hearts he was creating. Sally, the ever put-together professional, had to force herself to concentrate just a bit more when Ryan walked in.

Harlow watched the three sit expectantly, and loved everything about them. All so different, but all of them beautiful, passionate, and driven.

She'd heard friends and colleagues from other companies tell her that millennials were lazy and ruining their corporate drive. Harlow had seen first-hand that was far from true. She'd never seen individuals have so much fun and try so hard to produce results in her lifetime. They embraced the old, and she loved that they understood and drove them toward the new.

"Okay," Harlow began, "let's get started. It sounds like Jacquelyn is on track. Is there anything she needs from me that wasn't in her recap email this morning? Does she need any assistance in set-up or opening?"

"She is on top of it." Sally took the lead. "All decorations are in place. Props – like the wooden toboggan sleds and the hay bales for on-ice seating – arrived yesterday. Those should be in place by," Sally looked at her watch, more out of habit than a need to see it was ten after nine, "now."

Sally drew her chestnut hair over one shoulder, not realizing her nervous habit, and went on. "The food vendors are scheduled to arrive at five tomorrow morning. They are expecting a crowd. At least double what they had last year since it was such a hit. And it's the Saturday before Thanksgiving so it's anticipated that a lot of people won't be working next week. Jacq calculated for that, too."

"Perfect. Please let me know if you hear of anything from her. I know she'll reach out to one of you before me, but I'm available." Harlow nodded, took a sip of her coffee, and made a note that everything was on track. "Okay, Vanessa, how are you doing at the hotel?"

"Good. We are back on track after the delivery mix-up last week."

Harlow appreciated Vanessa's word choice. 'Mix-up,' to Harlow's mind, was putting it extremely nicely. The florist sent less than half of the greenery, garland, and poinsettia order. And what they did send went to the wrong hotel – in the wrong state. Apparently, Minnesota and Michigan were easily interchangeable.

Vanessa had simply gotten on the phone, redirected the shipment, got a refund for the undelivered items, covered the charge for the delivery, worked with a local flower and garden shop, and had the rest of the delivery the following Monday.

"I've confirmed with Sasha – the hotel's event planner – the room will be set up by tomorrow morning. We're talking over-the-top blues and silvers – on and in everything. Bulbs, flowers, tassels, vases, and even the food. The caterer is prepared and we've confirmed the headcount. Entertainment was set up last night and they'll arrive by three tomorrow. That's four hours before the seven o'clock start time. And their equipment – silver."

Vanessa looked around and saw her comment received smiles from the room. They knew it was ridiculous too, but it was just the right amount of obnoxious.

"Hors d'oeuvres will be served to the five hundred guests upon arrival – cute, dainty finger-foods. There will be holiday cocktails, beer, and wine available for beverages straight through the night. A plated dinner will be served at eight with light holiday music continuing to play in the background. At nine the dessert bar will be set up. The Bistro will provide the treats and do set up and break down. I've seen the spread – they look delectable. And if any of you make it, they are making extra dinner plates for emergencies, it's roasted rack of lamb with blueberry glaze." Vanessa moaned as she pretended to faint falling to the tufted back-rest. "There are no words."

"Music will pick up at that point, offering a more festive beat." Vanessa sat up and went on. "It will hopefully encourage dancing *and* for those in attendance to open their wallets. There is a raffle for prizes large and small. All proceeds going to Heritage House. It's an orphanage in downtown St. Paul."

Heartfelt *ahh's* made their way out of Sally and Ryan at the generous gesture.

Vanessa agreed and went on to tell the group it was the first party thrown by two accounting firms that joined forces in October. There were good feelings all around and she couldn't wait to celebrate with them – they'd invited her as a guest to her own party.

Ryan then lived his own bit of excitement as he recounted the details of his event taking place at the NHL hockey arena in St. Paul. It was all-man, or all-fan, appropriate.

Miniature hockey gear ornaments took over the trees that would be lit up all around the rink and near the concessions areas on every floor. Over four-hundred of them. Minnesota's team had donated signed jerseys, posters, sticks, and pucks to the event.

"Everything is good. The only thing I might need help with is the final walk-through for the charity executives. They are hoping for a picture at the opening of everybody who came together to make the event happen. Harlow, are you available for that?"

"Friday, December 13th?" Harlow asked, mostly for Ryan's sake, to let him dictate, but she knew their schedules inside and out.

"Nailed it. Could you be there around six?"

"Perfect."

Ryan smiled proudly, and Sally and Vanessa nodded at themselves for an update well done. Their pride lasted until Lisa, the busiest one of them all, ran into the room.

"Did I miss it? I missed it. Shit." Lisa asked and answered her own question, then plopped herself on the chair across from Ryan, and sank in exhaustion.

Harlow, and the rest, attempted to hide their amusement as they watched the new mom chug coffee like she would water after running a marathon through the snow. And by the look of her boots that hadn't yet been changed into heels, she might have done just that.

"I'll give you the update. Everybody is executing perfectly." Harlow sent appreciative and proud looks toward the group then continued, "We are on track and it seems it's going to be a very Merry Christmas."

"Thank God. What is Christmas again?" Lisa joked as she looked up, pretending to be confused, then added, "I'll meet up with each of you in our one-on-ones to make sure there isn't anything else you need from me, or last-minute details you'd like my help with."

"Sounds great, Lis." Ryan said, the first to get up and walk out with a wave, then he answered a phone call from one of his clients he greeted by name.

"Lisa, you're stunning. Even in your frazzled, no-sleep, new baby world. It's making you sparkle like a fresh, fluffy snow," Sally said as she followed Ryan out and tapped Vanessa on the shoulder, a sign that told her she should follow suit.

Vanessa stood, reached over to squeeze Lisa's hand, winked, and followed Sally. The women walked out organizing a trip to a coffee shop for their next meeting. And they'd need it seeing as they'd be putting in a long couple of weeks, and many days with hours that would reach well into double digits.

Harlow looked at Lisa and smiled sympathetically but with as much joy she knew Lisa's new baby brought into the world.

"How is sweet baby Layla?" Harlow asked.

"She's great. The most precious, unsleeping human on the planet."

"What if you just took a couple more weeks off. I promise we will be fine here." Harlow didn't have the heart to tell Lisa that when she was gone things trudged forward, but barely.

It was hard losing the one person who knew everybody's schedule; scheduled all the meetings, job interviews, client interviews; had relationships with the event planners from the hotels, local, and national caterers; knew where to get the best deals, and understood the ins and outs of tailoring your mood and correspondence to appeal to the right people for the right occasions.

"Not a chance. I need a break. Even if it is so I can sleep at my desk. But if it gets to that point, I promise I'll book one of the mother rooms. Might as well hook myself up to the pump if I'm going to be still for more than ten minutes," Lisa said, pointing to her boobs like they were feeding objects rather than an appreciated and appealing part of her body.

"Okay, but if it gets to be too much, you tell me. Before we get too into work, what can I bring for Thanksgiving?"

Harlow asked, excited about the holiday that was now only six days away.

"Yourself and your favorite bottle of wine. Nothing more, nothing less. You know how Mom and Steve get. They rule the kitchen and no outsider must enter."

Lisa and Harlow both understood the term 'outsider' was affectionately used for any person who wasn't her mom or her doting husband, which included family.

"Understood." Harlow saluted.

"Did you call them?" Lisa asked, changing the subject, knowing Harlow's family had been on her mind.

Harlow thought of them constantly, but more so around the holidays. Lisa knew the Hills came from money. She'd known since she and Harlow were childhood friends going to the same elementary and high schools. But as people do, they had drifted apart during college and the first couple of years back in St. Paul. It wasn't until Lisa had applied for the Executive Event Coordinator job that they had reconnected. They'd hit it off again immediately and filled a void in each other's lives they hadn't realized was missing.

When they rekindled their old friendship, Harlow had confided in Lisa that the money was still there, but the once-close family had begun to jet-set around the world and hopping around to live in different states. Vincent, Harlow's brother, had moved his wife, Catherine, to New York to open a branch of their marketing and advertising company there. And Harriett, her sister, had done the same but had taken her skills to Nashville. Her parents, Walter and Vivienne, had since retired and liked to spend the holidays in France, Italy, or any other picturesque European country.

This year, Harlow had waffled and wavered on reaching out to them to see if they'd all come home for Christmas to spend it together like they used to.

"I haven't." Harlow's head dropped, showing disappointment in herself and readied for a stern talking-to from Lisa.

Lisa got up and sat on the coffee table so she could sit and reach across Harlow's desk to take her hand.

"I promise it won't be hard. Just a quick call. Or even a text. Just send a quick feeler out there to get everybody's schedules?"

"It's not the schedules I'm worried about. And calling or texting isn't the hard part. It's the answer that I might get in response. I'm afraid to hear they won't be able to make it. Or, that they offer I go to them – which would be really nice – but it's not home." Harlow shook her head.

"I know. I understand," Lisa said, letting out a sigh for her friend. She understood, because even though her parents and extended family were always around and she had them for all holidays and special occasions, she couldn't imagine how sad she would be if one day she didn't have that. "But promise me you'll keep thinking about it. Your family is wonderful. I bet they just don't realize how much you all would love it. How much you all need it."

"I promise. Lis, you are amazing. And you do actually 'sparkle like freshly fallen snow.'"

The women laughed at Sally's description from the meeting, but only out of appreciation. And, if Harlow wasn't mistaken in her friend's glow, it was the truth.

CHAPTER 2

"Thanks, Brandon. Yeah, if you could have that ready by the time I get up that would be great. We aren't wasting any time on this."

Harris Porter stomped his boots, shook out his tailored winter coat, and tenderly smoothed and brushed the flakes out of his styled hair upon walking into the building.

He continued to listen to Brandon, his number one product manager, confirm he'd be able to have information ready on the feed company they were looking to collaborate with by the time he made it up to their offices.

Hopefully the collaboration he was working on would happen in the *very* near future. Very near if he could convince – probably more like beg – his dad. Maybe by the second quarter if he pressed hard. And fourth quarter if he let it happen organically and didn't come up against any hurdles along the way.

"Perfect. Just walked in. Be up in five," Harris said, before he swung the second set of doors open that led to the completely modernized Creamery, Co.

Harris looked around and smiled at the angled, black strips of wood that paneled the reception desk, noting it looked modern but balanced out the white walls and the concrete desk tops, floors, and pillars. It was a remodel his dad had let him take on only a couple years earlier. Now, it matched their website and appealed to the younger generation – who were going to be their new customer and employee demographic.

He grinned but was baffled by the thought that the 'younger generation' no longer included himself. There was an entire youthful generation coming up behind him. They were ready to work, and ready for their work to make the world a better place. That's why this feed collaboration was so critical to their success.

Yes, he thought, he'd use that in his pitch to his dad. Charles Porter had made his own father's creamery business into a billion-dollar company. Harris had helped Charles turn it into a multi-billion-dollar company. And there was so much more they could do.

Harris jumped at the clank that sounded from behind him. When he turned he saw two boxes, at least six-feet-tall, trying to cram through the oversized double doors.

"Wait, wait!"

Harris whirled around once more to see Nancy Lawson, their front desk receptionist yell, while waving her hands to try and halt the delivery man.

"Good morning, Harris. How are you today?" Nancy asked as she whooshed by.

"Great," Harris responded quickly, hoping to get it in before she was out of earshot. "How are you?" he asked, letting out a smirk knowing she was too nice not to keep the conversation going.

"Oh, really," Nancy huffed, "really great." She turned her head slightly and lifted her voice. "The kids and grandkids all made it in last night."

Nancy huffed out another couple of breaths as she and the delivery man continued to reach opposite sides of the box in their repeated attempt to find each other.

"Can you imagine, ten adults and seven kids, all under the same roof? For a month. More actually. They are staying until the New Year." She shook her head stopped her tilting and put up a finger in Harris' direction, showing she'd be right back with him.

"Sir," Nancy greeted the driver after hovering on one side long enough to finally catch him, "good morning to you. I hope you are doing very well. You are soaked to the bone. We'll have to get you some coffee or a hot chocolate. But before then," she continued without letting the driver respond – and he seemed okay with that as long as he got the hot chocolate, as that's when his eyes and eyebrows perked – "you'll have to take this back outside. We have a delivery entrance and it will be much easier for you there. I promise. No squeezing through doors or scuffing my floors. Once you have it in, you come find me, and I'll have a hot cup waiting for you."

"Yes ma'am." The young driver nodded, gave a little salute, and was pulling the gigantic boxes back out the small opening he tried to jam them through.

Nancy turned on a dime and Harris watched the fit grandmother of seven speed walk back to her throne.

"Nicely done." Harris said, genuinely impressed.

Nancy nodded firmly, but added a smile that let Harris know she was back to their original conversation.

"What are you all doing for the holidays?"

"I'm probably working straight through. We've got some big opportunities knocking on our door." Harris wasn't lying about either, there was a good chance he'd miss the holidays this year.

"Harris." Nancy's motherly tone sounded like his own mom's disapproval of his working habits. "You have to make time for the holidays *and* for family. It's what's most important."

"I am – I will," Harris agreed, but his agreement wasn't as truthful, "But this is setting us up for the future. We will never have a want in the world. And, we'll be helping a lot of people."

Nancy looked at Harris. He was the same age as her youngest son, and she adored him just as much. She, like Harris she supposed, remembered a time when his father, Charles, had been frugal and unwilling to spend any of their hard-earned money. Charles hadn't been much different than Harris himself. As a result, they'd grown up humbly. It wasn't a bad thing, but she imagined Harris had felt the impact and never wanted to say he couldn't afford something. Whenever she pressed, it was always 'one more deal' or 'one more sale or collaboration," *Then* there would be enough. *Then* he would settle down.

She wished she could shake some sense into him.

"As long as you promise to at least take the important days off. Thanksgiving, Christmas Eve, and Christmas day. If for no other reason than realizing that you won't have anybody to work with." Nancy smiled at the laugh she got out of Harris. "You have very kindly given the company twelve holidays and those are three of them. Four if you include the day after Thanksgiving – so you might as well add that to your list too."

"I'll do my best," Harris agreed. It was genuine, and it was true that he'd be hard pressed to reach anybody on those days. He'd think about it more seriously since she brought up that point. And, if he showed up to the holidays it would make his mom happy – and maybe make his dad loosen up to the feed collaboration idea.

"Hey Nance," Harris said, his curiosity getting the best of him, "what was in those boxes?"

"Oh, one of them was a big tree and as many lights and ornaments we could fit into the empty spaces. The other was a giant post box for your dad's *Postmark Christmas* campaign. It's so wonderful, that idea."

"Don't we have at least twenty other trees in storage?"

Without missing a beat and without giving the chance for him to argue, Nancy looked Harris in the eye and smiled sweetly, "Now, we have twenty-one."

Harris laughed and nodded, accepted that apparently one office building could never have too many Christmas trees, then waved and headed to the elevator to make his way to the top floor. A floor, he had noted earlier that morning, that was already decorated, and exploding with Christmas reds and greens.

CHAPTER 3

Snow had been scarce in early November, but the cool flakes that fell now warmed Harlow's heart as she watched them fall while rocking Layla in her second-floor nursery.

Lisa and Steve had decorated it with plush blankets, fuzzy animals in whites, tans, and browns, and soft gauzy curtains that were just the right amount of precious baby-girl. The delicate chimes of a *Baby's First Christmas* snow globe were already filling the sweet little room. Some things just couldn't wait, Harlow thought, as she closed her eyes and listened as Layla slept in her arms.

When the music stopped Harlow looked down and envied the peacefulness of the darling face as she slept. She could have put Layla down minutes ago but the feeling of holding the sleeping baby tugged at her heart and amplified her longing to love. So she would love, hold, and rock this borrowed baby even if only for another ten minutes.

When Harlow had finally separated herself from Layla she stepped out and stretched, thankful she'd decided on an oversized sweater for the day. She'd eaten more in that one

Thanksgiving meal than she typically did in a week. She vowed to never eat again as she pushed away from the table earlier. And wouldn't you know it, she was almost ready to go back for round two.

"If you're thinking what I think you're thinking, you go first, because then I won't feel as guilty."

Harlow laughed at Lisa's ability to read her mind and nodded as though she'd been caught.

"I can't help it. It was too good. I was actually wondering if I had it in me for seconds on green bean casserole and stuffing before dessert. That is just so disgusting," Harlow groaned.

"What do you think I was doing when you took Layla up? I snuck seconds so I could be ready for dessert by the time you got out. Now you have to do it just to make me feel better about myself." Lisa wrapped an arm around Harlow and they walked to the stairs together. "How'd she go down?"

"Like a doll. She's beautiful. Perfect and beautiful," Harlow said, thinking it was an understated version of the truth. Layla was even more than that – she was a precious gift. After years of trying without success, Lisa and Steve had been blessed with a miracle.

"I'll call you tonight when she's up at one and four, we'll see if you still feel the same way," Lisa said with an eyebrow raised, but her smile was full of pride and joy.

"Forever and always."

"Yeah, yeah. Do you think you'll stick around for the movie tonight? Mom said she was watching the baby so Steve and I are getting a two-and-a-half-hour night out on the town.

For a movie. With the rest of the family," Lisa said, slowly playing out the words to make it seem less exciting as the thought dragged on.

"As appealing as that sounds, I think I'm going to head home. I love the idea of sweatpants and curling up on the couch with a big blanket. And I know your mom already has leftovers packed up for me – the saint – so I'll shamelessly sit surrounded by reheated Tupperware and relish every minute." Harlow grew more excited as she foreshadowed her evening.

"You sure?"

Harlow knew Lisa was asking out of care and concern. Lisa knew going home might be hard, especially on the holiday. But she'd be fine. She might even work up the courage to call her parents or text her brother and sister something more than the usual *Happy Thanksgiving, I love you and miss you.*

"Definitely." Harlow was determined to be independent and find a place in her heart to love the holidays and be thankful for everything she had – not just the pieces of the family she didn't. Besides, she was luckier than most. She had a family. They might have been scattered around the world but she'd take that over any alternative.

"Okay, but if you change your mind, you know where we'll be. Now, let's sneak in and stuff ourselves some more."

—

The snow had left a sparkling dust of white on the sidewalks and streets. It found its way into the creases of signs and stop lights until wintery gusts of wind would come and swoosh it around to land in another nook or cranny.

The beauty of the street lamps had illuminated the ground, causing it to glitter as Harlow drove by. It had drawn her out into the evening for a walk on Grand Avenue after she'd made it home.

It wasn't late, maybe only six or six-thirty, but the sky was dark and she needed those street lamps to light her way.

Tomorrow, the sidewalk would be bustling with Black Friday shoppers loading up with gifts, and lining up outside of the delicious restaurants after working up a hunger from all of their racing around. She loved it here for that very reason.

It hadn't been hard to be the one to stay. To purchase the home that had been given to her and her siblings. It was the perfect house in the perfect neighborhood. Now, looking down the softly lit street that looked like a scene out of a 1940's Christmas movie, it reaffirmed her decision to stay.

But tonight, she'd had the same feeling that had been creeping in over the past couple months, a certain loneliness when she walked through the mansion. *The Hill,* she thought. An immaculate Victorian with endless charm and character.

Growing up it was her haven, her excitement, and her playful escape. That was when she shared it with her family.

The first couple of years after everybody had moved out were nice. She had redecorated, keeping only the furniture and paintings that had the kind of nostalgia that tugged at your heart when you sat on them or looked at it. Everything else – that wasn't of great value and nobody else wanted – was sold in an estate sale, with the profits donated to local charities.

All-in-all, Harlow considered it a win. But after the redecorating and making it her own, the walls seemed too hollow and she found herself longing to have people shuffling around the kitchen, kids running through the halls with their feet stomping and echoing from the floors above, and something other than a blanket keeping her warm at night.

Harlow wrapped her arms tightly around her body at the thought, and the brisk wind swirled around her. As she did, the world around her came back into focus and she noticed a red, round man, opening a box that was nearly the size of himself.

She walked the two short blocks to get closer. She wanted to see what Santa was doing out on Thanksgiving night. Surely Mrs. Claus wanted him home. Surely *he* wanted some of Mrs. Claus' cookies. Harlow chuckled at her thought and shook her head.

"Santa? Hello, can I help you?" Harlow asked, holding back a giggle at the round body tugging at the industrial staples holding the box together – in what seemed to be a steel hold.

"Oh!"

Santa jumped then actually gave a "Ho-Ho-Ho" – the closest thing she'd ever heard to the sound she imagined the real Santa would make.

"Well, didn't you give me a startle." Santa laughed, grabbing his belly. "I would welcome the help if you aren't too cold out here on this beautiful night. It's like the weather knew a little snow would make my day."

It had been a long time since Harlow had believed in Santa Claus, but this man might make her a believer once more. Everything about him was jolly; his voice sounded like a song, and his laugh hit his jiggling belly every time.

"Sure!" Harlow was delighted she could help. "What would you like me to do?"

"I think if you'd be willing to hold the box in place I'd get a good enough grip on it to get it open. It keeps skating in circles every time I try to pull it."

Harlow positioned herself next to Santa and readied herself to push so she could hold the box in position as he pulled.

"One, two-" Santa pulled on three and the staples sounded like tiny fireworks as they popped free from the side of the box. "We did it!"

Santa held his hand high for Harlow to slap it for five as they cheered.

"What's in here?" Harlow asked, trying to peek around the now opened flap.

"Oh, this? This is a miracle maker," Santa said as he rounded the box, removing the rest of the cardboard and foam. "It's a Christmas mailbox."

"For letters to send you?" Harlow could feel herself being drawn into Santa's excitement.

"For that and so much more. Some people, kids and adults alike, have no place to send their Christmas wishes. For things that are more than a gift you can wrap in a box. And sometimes you can't give your wish to a parent, or in some cases there aren't parents to help you send the wish."

Harlow covered her heart with her gloved hand as it broke while she listened and thought about those children who Santa was talking about.

"So, we set up this beautiful Christmas-red mailbox for any and everybody to write and send their Christmas wishes. Some things that are wished for can't be fulfilled, but we sure try our best to come close."

"I love everything about it. It's wonderful." Harlow brushed a small tear away from her blue eyes and pushed a stray curl of red hair behind her ear.

"It really is. Wonderful, that is," Santa agreed and looked at Harlow.

It wasn't the first time he looked at her but this time he stared, pleasantly it seemed, but knowingly, too. Like he saw her through and through.

"You know," he started, "Christmas is for everybody. Sometimes wonderful, magical things can happen by making a simple wish. Perhaps you'll be back. You never know what miracles Christmas can bring."

Harlow smiled at the wise man and his rosy-red cheeks and delicately wiped another tear away.

"Thank you, Santa. I just might."

Harlow leaned in, gave Santa a kiss on his warm cheek, and turned to head home. Thankful she was blessed enough to have   one.

CHAPTER 4

Harris had obeyed his mom's wishes and didn't talk about work once during Thanksgiving dinner, at all during dessert, and had waited until the last guest had left his childhood home.

He stood next to Barbara Porter now, wiping down the dishes she insisted on washing by hand. He wouldn't dare suggest his mom use the state-of-the-art dishwasher just to her left.

"I know what you're thinking," Barbara said, stealing a look at Harris.

"Whatever do you mean?" Harris said innocently, straightening his face and looking like he'd been caught. He knew his mom had always been able to read him as if he was a book she'd written herself. He smiled at the laugh he got out of his mom and prepared for her words.

"I know, it's the one day we have more dishes than we do in an entire month, but it gives me time to be thankful for all that we have."

Barbara handed him a white casserole pan to dry before she continued. "Harris, this family, this house – we are so lucky. So, at the end of a day like today, when we are all together, laughing and telling stories, I like to look out of this window that we were able to place here by design, and cherish every minute of washing these dishes. I'm also thankful that one of my children chooses to help me do it."

Harris grinned and bent down to kiss his mom on the apple of her cheek. He noticed the wrinkles that had formed lines across her cheek, and the way smile lines creased as her lips tipped upward and appeared in the corners of her eyes. In that moment, she was more beautiful than she'd ever been.

He'd inherited her height, her wide square frame, and her dusty blonde hair. 'It looks like a big pile of ash,' his mom used to say when she'd be prepping for a night out with his dad while curling her hair or wrapping it up high. More for laughs than vanity.

"You know, you can go talk to him now," Barbara said, not making eye contact, and instead smiling out into the wintery night as she wiped her hands with a dish towel embroidered with fall leaves and a funny looking turkey. She'd enjoy the happy rag today, because tomorrow they would be packed away and holiday towels adorned with mistletoe and holly would replace them.

"I know. I figured it could wait until I helped my mom with the dishes." Harris smiled sweetly.

"You're nervous, aren't you?"

"What? Of my own dad? No..." Harris paused, then sank. "Yes, absolutely. He's way too light and happy of a man. It completely throws off my handsome, go-getter-vibe I'm trying to emanate."

Barbara threw her head back and laughed. It was funny because she'd known it wasn't out of fear, but out of the drive and determination for the job that would clash against her husband's desire to have his employees – and his son – spend time with their families during this season. Barbara figured whatever was important enough for Harris to want to steal time away on Thanksgiving for, was probably the type of project that would consume their lives for a while.

"If it's for the right reasons, you know your dad. He'll listen and consider," she said gently, knowing her husband had once carried the same overzealous ambition her son had now.

Harris stared out of the window with his mom for a bit and thought about it. His dad would think about it. He would consider. Harris was worried about what his dad would do to make him work for it – to earn it. It wouldn't be the first time Charles Porter added a little something extra to his negotiations – and he usually got his way.

"Yeah. Maybe I'll talk to him Monday."

Barbara tipped the corner of her mouth up in a grin. "Why don't I make you your first hot chocolate of the season? You can wonder what your dad will bribe you with while you sip."

Harris thought about it, swayed his head back and forth, then agreed. "Yeah, sounds good." And a little of his mom's homemade hot chocolate never killed anybody, he thought. "But we're using the dishwasher for the new dishes."

"Deal."

It was his mom's turn to place a kiss on his cheek before she started to work on the thick, sweet chocolate.

CHAPTER 5

Harlow flipped her collar up and held it tight around her neck as she looked up at the picturesque Victorian that now looked like a scene from a Currier and Ives painting. It's as if the house knew that today the season had shifted. Autumn would be frozen beneath the frost of winter and it would transition from beautiful to magical.

The Hill stood with five stories of intricate design in classical white. Two cupolas and a belvedere sat atop a massive wooden-mansard roof, in fish scale shingles. Twelve dormered windows sat nestled into the roof, circling the top floor of the mansion. The space between the fifth and fourth floors offered hand-carved eave brackets that held the swoop of the roof as it elegantly sloped toward the street.

Harlow opened the iron gate that edged the front garden. The curved black iron was held in place by two stone posts, each with a luminous lantern welcoming her home and lighting her path forward. She looked up and noticed the light of the moon reflecting off of the endless windows stretching the length of the house and on each side – every window meant to be identical to the one a floor above it. But she knew the individual craftsmanship of each window would have all of them slightly different.

Her eyes followed the stone steps that would lead her up to the second-floor porch that circled the home, and the round pillars that added a touch of regal to the elegance.

Harlow moved forward, bypassing the steps, and pulled open the doors of the first floor instead.

Stacked sandy brown bricks acted as the support for the base of the home and held the historical plaque that gave the details of the home and its established year: 1898. The stone bricks were a sturdy contrast to the rest of the house's creamy white.

Harlow pulled the white wooden door open, stealing one final look out to the winter night, and walked in knowing exactly what she wanted to do tonight.

—

Wintery pine-scented candles were lit, hot chocolate was made, the fire was warming the den, and five boxes filled with at least ten photo albums, stray pictures, and drawings her parents had saved, had been hauled down from the attic. And, Harlow brought a bottle of red wine up from the cellar for good measure.

The first box opened, and she smiled at the musty paper smell that billowed to freedom. She brushed her hand along the edges of the first album and pulled it out. These were the boxes that held her Christmas memories. Nostalgia captured in glossy, aging color.

Harlow lifted the gold-trimmed album and rested it on the square coffee table that sat between three chesterfield leather couches and the wild flames of the carved fireplace.

As she opened the first pages she saw a Christmas tree three stories tall illuminate their foyer. She, her brother, and sister all dressed head to toe in red-printed and lace-trimmed dresses, and handsome sweater vests, smiling brightly while posing for pictures.

She laughed at the number of images that captured moments of distraction, goofy faces, and one of her sister who was barely holding in tears of exhaustion.

Leaning back, Harlow pulled the album to her lap and tucked her feet beneath her. As she turned the pages they bent in thirds, each third lined with the pictures in rows.

Her parents had captured images of Harlow and her siblings racing down the endless curved staircase to see what Santa had brought them. They had always received two small gifts and one that was a little less sensible and a little more extravagant.

Harlow smiled and admired her parents' excuse for not letting their children have whatever they wanted, whenever they wanted. They'd had the means, but they also realized having things wouldn't make them happy. Experiences would.

Harlow sat back.

Experiences, she thought. That's what her parents and brother and sister were doing right now. Living, experiencing.

She understood that, in a way. Not everybody could experience the world and life the way her family could. So they did, and they appreciated it.

But, Harlow thought, she wanted a different kind of experience. She wanted to experience sharing a life with somebody. She wanted to experience late nights with the love of her life as they rushed sleeplessly to a crying baby. *Or babies,* she thought with a wistful smile.

Staring at the images before her, Harlow sat up a little straighter and tried to fight off the thought that fluttered in and landed on her mind, like a snowflake would flutter and land on her lash.

"That's just ridiculous." She said the words to herself as she slid the album off of her lap to rest on the couch beside her.

Harlow lifted herself, listening to the creaks of the old wooden floor as her wool-socked feet moved her across the room to an oval, grand executive desk.

She pulled open one of the drawers in search of letter paper and a pen. Harlow stared at it for just a moment and looked around as if she'd be judged if she were caught embarking on this childish Christmas pastime.

Deciding she couldn't be judged if nobody was around to see it – and she was very much alone – she quickly grabbed the sheets of stationery and the pen, then scurried back to her warm cushion on the couch.

On a mission, Harlow pulled out her favorite Christmas and winter pictures, and scattered them on the table in front of her. She moved from album to album, laughing and smiling at the joy on the faces she'd seen too seldomly.

Tipping the final box, she realized she'd reached the end. Harlow fell back and brought her second glass of wine to her lips.

The table was filled with unhindered happiness.

Harlow scanned and pulled out a picture of her and Lisa sledding. Their bodies surrounded in puffy pink and purple jackets and matching snow pants. Their stocking caps sitting crooked on their heads. And their mittens covered in snow and hanging from strings that dangled from their sleeves.

She set it aside, wanting to frame it and give it to Lisa as a gift this year. A gift of childhood excitement and a foreshadow of all of the wonderful things to come with her daughter, Layla.

Then she looked down at the array of photographs in front of her. Each picture held a special place in her heart, but she searched for only the happiest memories. Ones she held in her mind and could see in bright, glittering colors. Ones that if given the chance to live again, she would in the swift jingle of a Christmas bell.

Harlow looked, raised, inspected, and shuffled. The pictures made their way to the left or right, until there were ten. Ten unforgettable Christmas memories. She held her body tightly and leaned forward, resting her chin on her hand as she looked. Yes, these were it.

Then she set her glass of wine on the table, picked up the paper and pen, rolled her eyes at what she knew was a wishful and ridiculous childish venture, and started writing.

Dear Santa,

Merry Christmas and a happy, peaceful holiday season to you.

"I can't believe I'm doing this," Harlow said, and leaned her head back, unable to fathom that she was writing a letter to Santa at thirty-two years of age. She sat up to take another swig of wine hoping for some liquid courage. She let the truth and sentimentality take her over, and lifted her pen once more.

I am not a person who is in need of anything in this life. I am blessed beyond measure. So please, if you must choose between this letter and ones of others, choose theirs. Their Christmas wish is much more important than mine.

However, if you happen to find some extra time, and feel like adding a little Christmas magic to my life, I would love for you to read this.

I would like experiences. Magical winter experiences. Inside are pictures of the best Christmas moments of my life, and I'd like to get to experience them once more. Here they are.

1. Find the perfect Christmas tree and decorate it

2. Decorate my entire house from top to bottom (this might not seem like an experience, but in the off-chance you haven't seen my house, just take my word for it)

3. Go ice skating

4. Take a walk in a winter park

5. Make Christmas cookies

6. Buy the perfect Christmas presents

7. Make homemade hot chocolate and watch an old Christmas movie

8. Throw a Christmas party

9. Be with the people I love on Christmas morning

10. Fall in love

Harlow looked at the last picture she'd saved. Her parents wrapped in each other's arms, twirling around the tree, embraced in a dance that was filled with love.

She remembered the scene like it happened only yesterday.

Vincent and Harriett had sat on either side of her as they stared through the spindled railing from two stories above. They whispered and giggled as they fought for position and who would get to use the new Nikon camera to snap a picture. Harlow had won the argument, and when they settled, they looked on as *White Christmas* quietly sang from the record player. She watched, then snapped a picture of the two people she loved the most in the world, hold each other closely.

Their movements had been like a ballerina gracefully circling in a snow globe, completely enchanting, with all the feelings of love.

She read through the list once more then shook her head. Love like that doesn't come from Santa Claus.

Harlow crossed out her last wish until it was unreadable, then signed the letter.

From a hopeful believer in the Magic of Christmas,

Harlow   *Hill*

CHAPTER 6

The weather outside was more than frightful; it was a wind-whipping, snow-pelting, face-burning blizzard of terror.

Harlow couldn't quite believe *this* was the day she decided to drop her letter off at the Christmas Postbox. *Seriously*, she thought to herself as she trudged up Grand Avenue, *you're crazy.*

When she reached the office almost an hour later, she decided the twenty-minute drive was worth it. Harlow could have stayed home, worked from her library, but she needed Lisa. When she ran by Lisa's desk, Harlow motioned for Lisa to follow her and yelled, "Christmas emergency!"

Lisa grinned and looked at Jacquelyn and Ryan who had taken in the sight of their boss – who had barreled into the office like the winter storm she'd just walked in from – and chuckled in return. Lisa grabbed her caffeinated lifeline and followed Harlow into her office and closed the door.

"You look," Lisa leaned her head to the right and took inventory, "like you've been through a Christmas blizzard."

Harlow paused her fuss over her desk where she'd thrown her bag and followed Lisa's eyes to the coat rack where her jacket wasn't neatly hung as it usually was, but tossed messily over the top so it looked like a snow-soaked tent.

"It's because there *is* a blizzard. Outside *and* in my brain." Harlow said in a whisper, not caring that nobody would have been able to hear her through the closed door anyway. Perhaps if she whispered, she wouldn't be admitting to herself, or her dearest friend, she'd written a letter to Santa Claus.

"I take it you didn't reach out to your family?" Lisa asked, already knowing the answer. If she had, Harlow wouldn't be frazzled, she'd either be delighted, or feeling dejected. Not...*this*. Which Lisa would describe as a Christmas lunatic packaged in pretty red-headed wrapping.

"I...reached out," Harlow said, and sat stiffly in her chair holding her head high, trying to force dignity. She pulled out her lipstick and reapplied the red while Lisa stared at her confused.

"You did?" Lisa let the words drag out. "To, your family?"

"Maybe not to my family," Harlow admitted.

"Oh God. You didn't reach back out to Andrew?" Lisa asked as she leaned forward, the fear evident in her voice.

"What? No!" The shock from the suggestion she'd reached out to her ex allowed Harlow to come down enough to take a breath. "Gross."

"Then I've run out of people that you could have reached out to." Lisa leaned back, resigned, and sat, waiting for Harlow to get a hold of herself and explain.

Harlow mirrored Lisa's actions and leaned herself back. She took a cleansing breath, went for it, then braced for impact.

"I wrote a letter to Santa." The delivery was flat and matter-of-fact.

"You," Lisa sat, wondering if she'd heard her friend right, "you wrote a letter to Santa? Like, jolly old Saint Nick? The man in the big read coat?"

"Yes," Harlow responded and added a slow nod after she spoke, as much to herself as to Lisa.

Lisa sipped her coffee and barely noticed the mint flavoring she'd added for a bit of Christmas spirit that morning.

"I don't mean to be the one to tell you this, honey, but I think you can stop worrying. I don't think Santa is real."

"He *is,* though."

The fictitious seriousness that had spread across Lisa's face only moments earlier shifted to a look of concern that said, *I'm going to need you to explain what you mean.*

Lisa wasn't quite sure if she was watching her friend take one step toward the loony bin, but she'd give it a little more time.

"Or, this one is," Harlow explained. "I took a walk Thanksgiving night because it was beautiful outside and I needed the fresh air. And the exercise." She thought back to the amount of food she'd eaten that day but decided she was allowed the day of indulgence.

"Anyway, I ran into Santa. He was setting up a cute Christmas postbox and said it's where people send their Christmas wishes."

Harlow pointed to her head to indicate she understood she was acting a bit bizarre, and went on, "Under normal circumstances I wouldn't have bothered because yes, *I know*, Santa is not real. But I know for a fact that these letters are read. *And* that they try to fulfill them. But you know, I shouldn't even worry about it. There have to be hundreds of letters that will have much more important wishes than mine. So, I bet they won't take the time."

"Ohh, interesting." Lisa nodded, letting the story settle. Then she nodded more fervently. "Yes. Interesting. Interesting, and I love it! I think it's a great idea."

"You what?" Harlow halted her own paper cup of coffee as it moved toward her mouth, it was her turn to be confused.

"Yes! I totally love it. You wrote down what you want most and put it out there. The universe *will* respond! Maybe, 'Santa,'" Lisa rabbit-eared quotes around the happy-man's name and continued, "will read it, and maybe not. But you took the time to put down what would make you happy at Christmas. It's brilliant. Everybody should do that – *I* should do that," Lisa added, nodding again, then continued. "I bet not a single thing on there was a gift, or some physical thing?" Lisa asked.

"You mean aside from a man?" Harlow added.

"You asked for a *man* from *Santa?*" Lisa assumed Harlow would pick up on the sarcastic disbelief dripping from her words.

"Pathetic, I know. I thought so, too. I crossed that line out. Nothing big, just things like a chance to decorate the tree and the house, and to be with the people I love on Christmas morning."

Lisa laughed and stood. "Sweetie, you are amazing. I love that you wrote Santa a Christmas wish. I'm sorry, I have a meeting coming up in a couple minutes so I have to get going, but I was just thinking: Why not do all of those things on your list? Nothing is stopping you from having a wonderful Christmas. If you don't want to reach out to family, you have friends all around you that would love to create and believe in the magic of Christmas with you. Decorate your house. Make plans with friends. Make your own wishes come true." Lisa smiled and saw that Harlow didn't know what to say, so she quietly turned and walked out of the office, closing the door behind her.

Left alone, Harlow thought about Lisa's advice. There really wasn't anything stopping her from doing all of those things.

She could call friends or neighbors over to laugh and sing along to Christmas songs playing on the radio while decorating and making Christmas cookies. It wouldn't be hard for her to stroll through a winter park with a steaming cup of sweet chocolate or rich espresso. She could skate along with strangers who were out enjoying the season just as she would be.

She could do all of those things. She *would* do all of those things. Sure, when writing her Christmas wish she had envisioned doing all of those things with a man, but how unrealistic was that? You actually *needed* a man to do those things *with* a man.

So, she thought, resigned but determined, she would do all of those things by herself. She'd invite people when she could, and enjoy every single moment of it.

CHAPTER 7

Harris rose from his desk, looked at Brandon, and waited for his response.

He'd just reviewed the ability to join forces with Pro Feed – Minnesota's largest feed company – for a national effort to introduce technology that would make processes more efficient and profits increase for the farmers and the companies in the agriculture business.

To Harris' mind it just made sense and it fit nicely with their company profile. The technology they were talking about would blend high quality ingredients for the nutrition animals needed to sustain a healthy life. In turn, it improved the quality of the products those animals produced like meat, milk, and eggs.

It's also where Harris saw their company going in the near future. They'd begun in the dairy business, expanded to crops, and could see the benefit to potential customers and to them, if they built this relationship.

"Yes, it makes sense. The collaboration and direction. I can start working with experts. Do we have a budget, a timeline?" Brandon asked, knowing the budget wouldn't be a problem. The timeline? That could vary. But *the man*...the man might be a problem.

Brandon had seen Harris push for overreaching progress only to have his father, Charles Porter, slow his initiatives. Though, to Brandon's mind, they always seemed to find a place in the sweet spot where progress met delivery, and they hadn't missed an opportunity yet.

"I'm not worried about budget." Harris grinned to Brandon, knowing he knew that. "The timeline will depend on the *big guy*. That's where I'm headed now. If you like the idea though, don't be afraid to start progress. It's not if, it's when."

Brandon nodded and retreated to his own office and left Harris alone for one final independent-pep-talk.

"Okay, here it is. This is a big collaboration. Like billions of potential dollars. No pressure." Harris spoke to himself as he straightened his tie in the whitewashed reflection his office window provided.

He noticed the snow and the wind hadn't stopped whipping. That, he thought about the snow, would probably play to his disadvantage. A blizzarding reminder to his dad that they were moving head-on into the holiday season. His dad wouldn't like that he was pulling himself or their staff into the heavy workload the collaboration would bring.

Charles was on the phone when Harris knocked on his door, but it didn't matter; he smiled and waved Harris in enthusiastically. Harris sat in the simple wooden chairs his dad had insisted on keeping during the remodel. He rubbed a hand over the shiny brown he used to sit in as a child and grinned.

The knock on the door pulled him away from his memories, and he couldn't help but keep the grin when he saw Santa waving a chubby hand on the other side of the glass door. Harris and his dad waved him in simultaneously and Harris stood to offer a handshake.

Santa moved a red, velvet letter bag from his right hand to his left and took Harris' hand in the jolliest shake it's ever had.

"Harris!" Santa belted, "How are you doing young man? It's been, well, a year I suppose!"

Energy and happiness filled all of the empty spaces in the room as Santa laughed in his deep *Ho-Ho's.*

"I am doing great. It's good to see you. You're looking rather jolly. What have you got here?" Harris greeted and asked, motioning to the red bag.

"Oh this!" Santa lifted the bag high, "This is the first of the letters from the Christmas postbox. Can you believe it? A whole bag already. I just picked it up but wanted to make sure I knew where to deliver them."

"Good question – that is a question for the big boss," Harris said jokingly, "I'm the little boss. I don't get to make big decisions like those of Christmas letters. But let's see some of them."

Harris sat again in the wooden chair and Santa did the same, while pulling out some of the letters and setting them on the round table between them.

Most of the writing was the same, Harris mused. Words made up of letters of different sizes and colors. Pictures of Christmas trees, stars, presents, and rocking horses drawn in crayon-covered envelops of every color. They were happy and hopeful letters and drawings, but he couldn't help the trace of sadness some of the letters held.

Some would ask for presents. But others? Others would ask for family members to heal, moms or dads to come home, a job for their parents, to stop being bullied at school, or something as innocent as a warm place to sleep at night.

But they would help. Every single one of the letters would be answered in some way, and help offered in some form. They had volunteers, employees, companies, shelters – all ready and wanting to give and to help. Yes, he thought, something would be done.

"Thanks, Dear. Yes, yes, I know. Harris is right here."

Harris looked up at the sound of his name and he realized his dad had been talking to his mom on the phone the whole time. "I'll tell him. Okay, I'll be ready. Yes. Don't worry. Five o'clock. Yes. On the dot. I love you, too. Bye."

Charles Porter hung up the phone and beamed. He recapped his conversation while moving around his desk to get a look at the letters.

"My wife doesn't seem to think I can be on time, for anything, much less the play tonight. We are going to see *Holiday Inn.* She's got a thing for Bing!" Charles laughed at his rhyme and it was contagious.

"We have all of these already? Amazing. I can't wait to read them. Think of the things we'll be able to do for these kids," Charles said as he eyed the pile and reached in pulling out an envelope that had "Santa" written in cursive. He walked it back around his desk and sat once more.

"These you can leave here. We'll get them down to Nancy, but I'd like to read a few from this pile first. These letters make me long for a simpler day. I think," Charles addressed Santa, "the rest can go right to Nancy, as she's coordinating with the readers who will get the letters to the right people. But whenever you come in for a drop-off, head on up and we'll have a nice coffee or winter drink of your choice."

"I love the sound of all of that." Santa stood and took off his hat, revealing a head full of thick white hair. "A Merry Christmas to you both. We'll see each other again before Christmas, but I love the way it sounds. And Christmas isn't so much a day as it is a season anymore, is it?"

With that, Santa walked out, sent a final wave, and was gone.

Harris stared after him and spoke to the door, but for his dad to hear. "I think he's the real Santa. Yes," Harris nodded, "definitely the real one."

Charles laughed again and agreed, taking the credit, "I wouldn't dare to bring in anything but the real thing. So, son, what's on your mind? You have that look in your eye and you just got back from the Agriculture and Feed Conference. Let's hear it."

It wasn't necessarily a bad thing having a dad that knew you better than you knew yourself, but it definitely took away the element of surprise when he'd had that intention.

"We've talked about it before – the feed business I mean – and I think now is the time. We have an opportunity to collaborate with the leading Minnesota business – Pro Feed –

and if this goes well, I think we could add a four-billion-dollar business to our name. What do you think?"

Harris tried not to sound too hopeful, to remain steady and firm, but this excited him. He heard it slip into his voice as he asked for his dad's opinion.

Charles nodded slowly. He didn't disagree with his son. In fact, he wholeheartedly agreed. It wouldn't only be a great move, it would improve economics in the farming world by leaps and bounds. His own grandfather was a dairy farmer so the idea tugged at his heart a little more than it should have.

"What's the timing you had in mind?" Charles was ready for anything that implied 'as soon as possible' but he asked anyway.

"As soon as possible."

Harris watched his dad try and mask a grin.

"I'm going to need a little bit more," Charles admitted. "I want two things – and it shouldn't be trouble because I am sure you already have Mr. Carlson working on it."

Harris tried not to give away that he'd done just that and had Brandon begin work on it before walking in.

"One, I want all of the details of the collaboration. What you're thinking in terms of partnership. Bring in our lawyers, I want to make sure anything we put in a contract won't hurt our ability to buy, whether it's them or a different company, should we pursue this. That is, where I assume, you were going with this?"

"It is." Harris confirmed.

"Okay, then let's get a meeting on the calendar to discuss long term strategy. You know who to invite."

As he was speaking, Charles had begun opening the Christmas postbox letter. He knew from the swirly script on the front of the envelope that it couldn't have been from a child, and his curiosity had gotten the best of him. He let Harris wait as he continued to read the letter.

It was simple, and seemed like it came from a nice woman. He wouldn't have been able to know how old she was and he didn't seem to mind. He noted, and appreciated, everything she listed in the letter that she wanted didn't come in a box. As he opened the bottom of the letter pictures fell to the desk.

Harris walked up to look at the pictures and smiled at the old photos. They didn't look much different than the ones their family had taken when he was a child.

Both of the men allowed the hint of laughter to bubble out. Then Charles saw the sparkle in his son's eyes and decided he didn't give him nearly a hard-enough time since he was getting his way with the feed collaboration.

And, he assumed Harris would work straight through the holidays without taking time to enjoy it, which worried Charles that his son wouldn't experience the season's true magic.

Yes, Charles thought, a little decorating and ice skating might just do his son some good.

"No. Oh no." Harris said, seeing the same glint in his father's eyes. "I know what you're thinking. No, no. No." His hand flatlined as if to say *that's the end of it - no.*

"I'd like to amend my original instruction," Charles said, loving his new idea while picking up the pictures and stacking them so he could neatly place them back in the folded letter and hand it to his son.

"Dad, come on." Harris pleaded.

"If you fulfill this lovely woman's Christmas wish, *then* you can schedule the strategy meeting."

"Dad." Harris knew he sounded like a teenager who didn't get his way but he didn't care. He didn't have time for this.

"That's it, take it or leave it. I think I was rather generous letting you continue progress on the collaboration." Charles answered cheerfully.

Harris knew when his dad thought he was being clever and funny. If he argued, his dad would *clever and funny* his way into making him wait on the collaboration too. That wasn't a risk he was willing to take.

"Fine." Harris sighed as his head fell back and his eyes closed. When he lifted his head, he saw his dad proudly smiling at him.

"The feed collaboration is a great idea. I'm proud of you, Harris."

He knew his dad meant it.

"Thanks, Dad. Have fun at the play tonight. I'll be back later to remind you to leave so you can be on time – for once."

It was Harris' turn to carry a smug grin. When he heard his dad laugh and nod knowingly, he turned toward the door to give Brandon the news. And, to do a little research on his newest assignment.

The sooner he finished with the Christmas wish lady, the sooner he could get started on more important things.

CHAPTER 8

"Just reach in, get the letter out, go home, and make your own Christmas magic. Make your *own* magic. Your. Own. Magic," Harlow mumbled to herself while rummaging through a bin full of winter boots in her basement, scrounging to find a matching pair.

She saw the familiar top of a boot matching one she'd already pulled out and set aside, latched onto it, and pulled. When she yanked the boot to freedom, Harlow let out a squeal as she fell backwards with the momentum.

She slid on the boots from where she'd landed on the floor and tugged on her red knit hat and matching gloves. By the time she reached the first floor, she was sweating from head to toe.

As she opened the door, the burst of cold air rushed in and relieved her of the unwanted warmth. Harlow paused and looked at a scarf hanging on a nearby hook and grabbed it, knowing it would only take seconds for her sweat to turn to ice and she'd be back to freezing as she had been earlier that day.

Then she made her way through the foot of snow that had fallen, to the Christmas postbox she'd dropped her letter in earlier that morning.

—

Harris sat in his SUV. He'd parked it next to the postbox and left it running while he sat inside. He had an address, but he wasn't quite sure how to start fulfilling the needs of a woman he didn't actually know.

He flipped through her pictures again. He'd shuffled through them most of the day. He assumed Harlow – the woman who had sent the letter – was the redhead. She was the only one who was consistent in all of the pictures. Except for the last one. They, he could only assume, were her parents, and the ones responsible for the laughter on the kid's faces in all of the pictures.

Harris looked at them dancing and it tugged at his heart. Mostly, he decided, because it reminded him of his own parents. They shared a love like that.

Harris flipped through the pile of pictures once more and held one of three kids standing on chairs next to their parents close to his face. They were in a line along the kitchen island making something that required flour, he noted, as the white powder was dusted over everything – hands, cheeks, and hair.

"Vincent, Harlow, Harriet, Vivienne, and Walter." He squinted and read the names stitched onto the sweaters that would take first place in the ugly contest every time. Brother, two sisters, mom, and dad, he assumed. And confirmed Harlow as the red-head.

Harris laughed at the picture and looked up. When he did, he saw a woman high-stepping through the snow like she was walking over track hurdles, and his amused snicker lingered. Her head and face were covered in red wool. He wondered if she could even see through the tiny slit she'd left for her eyes.

The woman lifted and stomped her way past his parking space on the side of the road and stopped at the shiny red mailbox.

"Well isn't this something." Harris chuckled out the words as he watched the woman look around, pull down the red hatch, and reach her arm inside.

For a moment he felt bad for the woman. Clearly her depth perception was a little off, seeing as there was no way her arm would reach to the bottom of the box. But, he thought giving her the benefit of the doubt, he supposed he would have tried the same method if he wanted to get something out of there.

Now *that* was an interesting thought: don't people usually want to put letters *in?*

Harris set the letter and pictures aside, then opened his door as the woman rounded the box and crouched down behind it. He looked up and down the sidewalk, crossed it, and poked his head around the mailbox where the woman was hovering.

"Can I help you with something?" Harris asked, delighted at the comedic scene he was witnessing.

The woman screamed and jumped. She lost her balance and landed her bottom in a big pile of snow that had been plowed off the sidewalk.

"No!" Harlow yelled at the shock of getting caught then regained a little of her composure and tried again, "Sorry, no thank you."

Harlow lifted her head to get a better look at him but she couldn't see him – or anything – since the fall had scrunched her hat and scarf together covering her eyes completely. Her gloved hands lifted her hat and pulled down on the scarf.

When she got a clear picture of the man standing before her she realized had it been any other person she wouldn't have been embarrassed. But, she had fallen over in front of a cute blonde-haired man in a tailored, black wool jacket and nice leather gloves. So, she felt the embarrassment take her over.

"Here, let me help you up," Harris offered, holding out a hand for her to grab.

She agreed and popped up so they were standing face-to-face – then he saw it.

The same bright blue eyes he'd seen in the pictures, only instead of the young girl, he was staring at the woman she'd grown up to be. And, now that he was getting a better look, he saw the same strands of red curls spilling out from beneath her hat and scarf.

So, this was Harlow Hill, he thought, and she was – it seemed – trying to get her letter back.

"Harris Porter." He offered his hand for a shake and noted aloud, "And, people usually put things *in* the Christmas Postbox, yet it seems to me you are trying to get something out."

Her eyes widened, snapped to his and locked. She'd been caught, but there's no way she would admit to it.

"What? No, I was just – ah – making sure there wasn't any way the letters could fall out."

Really? she thought, wanting to roll her eyes as she searched for more words to say. "It's a big deal. This time of year, I mean." She stood tall and aimed for defending Christmas's honor. "So, this," she thumbed her gloved hand in the direction of the red box, "is totally important. Needs to be secure."

Harlow affirmed her words by slapping her hand on the side as if she'd inspected its solidness and approved.

"Is that right?" He only gave time for her nod. "Well, yes, it's good you're here to check on it. I wouldn't want any of the letters in there getting into the wrong hands. Christmas wishes are a serious matter."

Harris rubbed his hands together and smiled. He wished he could see her whole face, to see what had become of the girl whose laughter and smile illuminated the pictures on the passenger seat of his vehicle.

Harlow couldn't do more than stare. When – what was his name? Harris? – smiled, she'd lost her train of thought.

He was broad, she noted as her eyes fixated on him. He wasn't slim, but he wasn't big either. A hockey player maybe, she thought. Not now, but once. Or, that's how she imagined him. He probably had longer hair then. Somewhere between then and the fancy black clothes, he'd probably trimmed the unruly blonde ends to become the professional he was today. Harlow smiled at the made-up image she'd painted of him.

"Do you want to put a letter in for Santa?" Harris asked, he figured it was only kind of cruel to make her talk about it.

"I already – what?" Her attention flew back to face. "No, no. This is for kids. You know, they make wishes, lists, write them down, throw them in here." Harlow mimicked the act of writing as she explained and felt only a little ridiculous and over the top. "Its really not for adults."

Her head kept its back and forth motion, reinforcing her denial. "Okay then, I should probably get going, I'll just–" She tried to find a way out of the snow bank and realized she was blocked in by Harris, "step aside." She tried to maneuver around him but he didn't move.

"Sorry, I don't recall getting your name," Harris said, unmoving.

"Oh, right. I don't think I said it." Harlow tilted her head and tried to think back to all of the rambling she'd done in a surprisingly short amount of time. "Ah, Harlow. Harlow Hill. Nice to meet you."

At her forward motion he stepped back. He wouldn't have let her go so easily but he quickly realized if he wouldn't have moved she would have stepped right on him.

Harlow slid and shuffled a little bit as she hit a slick spot of sidewalk hidden by the fresh snowfall and caught herself with her arms and legs wide. When she got her balance she stood and turned back to him, and pulled down her scarf.

"It was nice to meet you, Harris. Have a Merry Christmas." She smiled at the handsome man she left behind and meant every word. And, she thought, having to forget about the letter she'd never get back, now she'd head home to take Lisa's advice. She'd make some Christmas magic all by herself.

Harris repeated her words, "Have a Merry Christmas." As they were the only words he could get himself to say.

When he'd seen her face, he realized the young enchanting girl from the photos had grown into a beautiful and stunning woman.

Her eyes and face were the shape of almonds and her lips were full and pink. Her blue eyes popped on her creamy skin that had the faint trace of freckles scattered across her nose and cheeks.

A tiny snowflake began freezing a spot on his nose and was enough of a startle for him to shake his head and pull himself out of the trance.

Huh, he thought, walking back to the SUV that was still running. Harris slid into the driver seat and picked up the envelope. He pulled out the letter, started to read, and looked at number one:

1. Find the perfect Christmas tree and decorate it

"The perfect Christmas tree? That's impossible," Harris said to himself. Everybody knew there wasn't *one* perfect tree. It all depended on style, tree-taste, and smell.

He'd have to go a different route.

Harris folded the letter and stuffed it into the envelope. He put his car in drive and drove to the nearest tree nursery.

CHAPTER 9

The boots, hat, gloves, and jacket were left in a heap by the first-floor door. Harlow was on a mission and didn't have time to deal with petty things like keeping a tidy house. Until tonight, she thought as she stared back at the mound, when she'd come back and pick it up. If she didn't, it would haunt and nag at her mind until she did it. So she stopped, turned back toward the mess, and picked everything up.

Harlow hung her jacket and scarf, stashed her hat and gloves in an old wooden storage bench, and moved her boots to rest on the tray next to the door.

She hated to acknowledge the satisfied feeling. Her parents' insistence on keeping a tidy house was loathed as a child, but she had to admit now – even when she hated picking up and putting away – the house was more enjoyable when it was clean. Walter and Vivienne Hill had successfully molded her into a tidy adult. They'd insisted a well-kempt home allowed the history to be preserved, and of course, the beauty of it to take center stage.

Harlow marched up the stairs to the first floor sitting room and opened the old record player. She fingered through the pile of records that sat beside it and pulled out Frank, Dean, Bing, and all of the other Christmas records she could find. Harlow placed Bing's *Merry Christmas* vinyl on the record player, and let the same *White Christmas* song her parents had listened to when they danced echo throughout the house.

Harlow moved from window to window and opened the drapes that had been closed the night before. With each opening it framed a new picture of the outside snow.

She paused and turned, then looked at the expansive house. This task called for a little strategy.

There were big boxes downstairs that held all of the decorations for the basement, first, second, and third floors. It also had the artificial trees for the fourth and fifth floors.

Then there was the attic. The attic had the remainder of the decorations for the fourth and fifth floors. Those would be easier to get down but maybe less important in terms of floor decoration.

So, she decided, she'd start with the basement, first, and second floors. And, she thought, she'd add her bedroom on the fourth floor to the list. She could hardly expect herself to fall asleep at night without the glow of a Christmas tree. She was making herself a magical Christmas after all.

There was a "servants' entrance" at the back of the basement. Seeing as her family had hated the idea and everything it stood for, they started using it as storage.

Harlow stood, staring at the monstrosity of boxes lining walls and piled high, one on top of the other. The sight was enough to discourage even the most motivated of Christmas enthusiasts.

But this was more than motivation. This was desire mixed with determination. She couldn't – wouldn't – be stopped. Christmas *would* be magical – regardless of the sore leg muscles and sweat that would drip from her brow.

When she found them, Harlow gripped the sides of the first box and wide-armed it to the base of the stairs and looked up. The box read *First Floor*. That's doable, she thought, then trudged up.

By the time she had six of the seemingly endless mounds of boxes distributed to their respective floors, she was grateful when the doorbell rang. Harlow rolled up the sleeves of her oversized blue button-down, tightened the hair in her high pony, and swung open the door, letting the freezing air breeze a welcome draft over her body.

"Hi, how can I help you?" she asked the man who was standing with his back to her, his body slowly spinning in a circle. He was taking it in, she thought. It wasn't an uncommon reaction to standing on top of the stone steps of The Hill. More than once when she'd opened the door she'd been greeted with a back or a bewildered profile taking in the property.

When he turned, his smile and his eyes held a bit of shock and awe. It was the only thing that kept her from melting, even in the frigid cold.

"Hi." Harris leaned back and broke eye contact to look the length of the house in both directions. When his stare came back to her he asked, "Remember me?"

It was Harlow's turn to smile. "I do. Should I be worried that you followed me home?"

"Ah, no, or, I don't think so. Unless you still want your Christmas wish back? Then I can leave." Harris thought about the deal his dad had given him, "But I don't really want to leave."

"My Christmas wish?" Harlow looked down, searching, then looked up, the realization hitting her as she asked the question. *"You* are the one that got my letter?"

Humiliation for the letter and the episode they'd had at the Christmas postbox had her head falling back and her eyes rolling.

Her actions allowed him to regain a little of his composure. Harris didn't want to think it was the most attractive bout of embarrassment he'd ever seen, but it was hard to push the thought away.

"So, your Christmas wish. I figured there's no possible way I could pick out the perfect tree, so I went for a wreath instead and figured we could go find a tree together. But," Harris' eyes stole another look at the house, "I didn't realize you had more than one door. Five of them, actually. Sets. Five sets of doors."

"Ten," Harlow corrected absently, and continued to explain as his face registered the news. "The floor below." She explained as if she'd been asked the details of the house her entire life and had it memorized. "They aren't identical, but there are matching doors below us. Anyway–" she took a minute to take him in and to analyze the situation.

She could turn him away and forget all about her letter and go on through the holiday season doing exactly what she'd set out to do – embark on her own magical Christmas experience – or? *Or*, she repeated to herself, thinking on the alternative.

Harlow took in the beautiful wreath he'd brought to her door with bright red berries and crispy brown pinecones bunched in threes, and the thoughtfulness behind it. And, it was true, finding the perfect tree was hard.

"The wreath is perfect," Harlow decided. "And the one you brought is beautiful. Do you want to come in?"

"Just like that?" Harris was shocked it had been that easy. How often does a beautiful red-head take your words for what they were and invite you into their Victorian mansion?

Harlow thought about it, but it didn't take long. "Yes. Just like that," she confirmed, moving aside to let him through.

"Okay," Harris said, sliding sideways through the door with the wreath pressed against his body. When he entered he was hit with Dean Martin bellowing *Winter Wonderland* and nearly gasped.

The house was a wonderland all its own, and it had nothing to do with Christmas. Just simple magnificence in size, craftsmanship, and disbelief that somebody could live in a home this extravagant.

The urge to wander wasn't hindered by respect or manners, it was the shock that rendered him immobile.

Harris held onto the wreath, at first because he couldn't move, but then because he didn't know if he was allowed to set it on the creamy marble floors that rounded the foyer. His body turned with the curve of the floors and took it all in – or as much as he could see from his three-sixty view.

A grand staircase boomed gloriously in the center of the room, the bottom of the steps nearly spanning the entirety of it only to trim into a smaller width as they reached the second floor. The bulky pillars that marked the end of the railings were a rich, espresso stain.

The same wooden-style was carried throughout. It was on all of the doors, archways, corners, and – upon looking up – a breathtaking domed ceiling.

Harlow walked over and held out her hands, a silent offering to take the wreath. She understood the brilliance of walking into her home. She loved it, but not boastfully. She loved it because of the magnificent history, beauty, and wonder that took people over and sent them into a dreamy trance. She would never get over the look of awe in the bright sparkling eyes and the bemused, amazed faces as they walked in.

Harris had seen money. He thought he had a lot of it himself. But this? This was entirely different. This was *wealth*. Wealth passed on from earlier generations. Generations that lived in a different world, a different era. Where luxury was displayed, and no expense was spared even on the most frivolous of details. And she lived here. Alone.

She lived here alone?

Harris turned and saw her peaceful, appreciative face smiling at his. He'd nearly lost his train of thought at her adoration. "You – ah – you live here? Alone?"

She hoped he didn't see the twinge of sadness that fought to break free when he'd emphasized *alone*. Instead

Harlow tried to hold onto appreciation and went for matter-of-fact. "I do. My grandparents inherited it from their parents. My parents inherited it from them. We inherited it from our parents. And I was the one that wanted to stay."

"We?" he asked, finally able to take a step toward the wandering he'd been drawn to since he'd entered.

"My brother and sister. My brother moved to New York and my sister moved to Nashville."

Harris nodded, and mentally placed the two from the photos he'd studied. He also noted the hint of longing in her voice as she described just how far away they were from her.

Be with the people I love on Christmas morning.

He thought of her letter and recalled her wish. When he did, a feeling of warmth he hadn't known was there wrapped around his heart, and for the first time in his life he had the urge to wrap someone else's heart with it. He wondered why that was? He'd just met Harlow Hill and he was already feeling like he wanted to take away her loneliness.

He didn't stop taking the house in as his mind wandered. He noticed the glamour of the home, but also noticed the emptiness.

Well, he thought, for nine – almost ten, noting the last wish was crossed out – Christmas wishes, she wouldn't be alone. They might as well get started.

"Where do you usually put your tree?" Harris asked, not having to try as hard as he thought he would for excitement.

"Which one?"

He laughed at the innocent way she'd asked and wondered just how interesting this was going to be.

"How about the ones that you'll see the most?" he offered, thinking she might as well get as much enjoyment out of them as possible. It was supposed to be magical after all.

Harlow took care with her thought. "This one." She bounced to the middle of the foyer, "The one that goes right here," pointing to where she stood. "And, one in the living room, next to the kitchen. Well, I guess technically it's the great room. And," Harlow felt embarrassment when his amused eyebrows wrinkled his forehead as they lifted, "my bedroom."

"Okay." Harris nodded slowly, taking in her selections.

"Okay?" Her response was tentative as she eyed him to see his response to her over-the-top decorating demands.

"Yes. Okay. Should we do it?" Harris asked. He didn't want to admit it, but the excitement he felt was growing.

"Really?" Harlow couldn't contain herself. "You're really going to help make my Christmas wish come true?"

"I am."

Harlow tried to keep the jitters from jumping out but she couldn't hold it in. She ran toward Harris and flung her arms around the stranger that was answering her Christmas wish. Happy tears welled in her eyes as she relished the warmth of the hug he'd wrapped around her in return, and for the Christmas memories she'd be able to live once again.

CHAPTER 10

The blizzard was over. The snow had stopped and the winds had slowed to quick, soft bursts that whisked the loose powder into glittery swirls. But what had remained was a white cloak of wonder that draped over the forest green of pine. It turned the tree nursery into a woodland wonderland.

They'd examined, compared, measured, analyzed branch sturdiness – and had an apple cider, hot chocolate, and mini-donuts.

An hour later they high-fived after picking out the perfect, fat Balsam Fir for her bedroom. One that would smell of deep, fragrant pine. They had leaned left, right, and circled a wide, long bristled Scottish Pine, perfect for hanging hundreds of ornaments on its sturdy branches for the great room. And they'd navigated through snow and needle-covered paths toward a sign that told them they'd find the trees over twenty feet tall if they followed the path lit by garland-adorned lantern lights.

"A twenty-foot tree?" Harris asked just to make sure she wasn't going a little holiday crazy.

"At least," Harlow deadpanned. She wasn't joking, nor was she going crazy. "It's an elegant, massive space. It deserves a tree that has a like description."

"How do you expect to get it inside the house?" he asked slightly worried about the top of his SUV and the two other trees that were already claiming the space. And, he thought, his manhood as he would try and struggle something that huge into place.

"They'll bring it to us." Her words were simple and she didn't give his question a second thought. She simply continued along the path, walking beneath the arbor that would lead them into the giant forest of trees.

"They'll bring it to us. *Of course,* they will," Harris mused to himself. "Why wouldn't your twenty-foot Christmas tree be delivered? Completely normal." Then he followed her, as he had no choice but to pick out an *elegant and massive* tree.

They weaved and wandered while they looked the trees up, down, and around.

"Aren't they beautiful?" Harlow asked as she stopped and gracefully grazed her hand across one of the trees pokey needles. "And the smell." She breathed in, inhaling the wonderful pine. "It's my earliest Christmas memory."

Harris didn't interrupt, he just watched her lids gently close over the glistening dark blue her eyes had taken on as day turned to night, and listened.

"I remember feeling like I was going to burst I was so excited. I couldn't sit still. My mom told me I looked like a rocket ship about to launch into space." Harlow stole a look at Harris and grinned, not embarrassed at the recollection, but innocent in describing her youthfulness. "Vincent and Harriett, too. It was our favorite night. More even than Christmas morning. We were going to Grandma and Grandpa's house – The Hill – for the Christmas party," she explained, circling the same tree. "It was more than magical. It was enchanting. The whole house turned into a dream. A Christmas Eden. Golds and silvers seemed to burst like starlight, and cranberry reds and emerald greens danced as I would twirl circles in every room."

Harlow grabbed Harris' hand and spun beneath it, lost in her story and enchanting him as he imagined she was enchanted in her memory. He listened to her laugh as she spiraled away from him and wondered if he'd ever felt that happiness.

"Gold carts with mirrored trays held punch and eggnog in crystal bowls, and silk-clothed tables held savory meats, elegant sides, and more Christmas desserts and treats on silver platters than any child should see."

Harlow paused and looked down, and let a sweet curl twist her lip upwards, "But even with all of that, what I remember most of all is the way the beautiful tree smelled of pine and fresh winter snow."

Harris moved to her, wanting to take her hand as she stood, but he resisted and his body stopped next to hers as she looked up to him, then to the tree.

Of all the memories, he thought, the extreme stimulation of senses she experienced as a child – and that he could almost feel in her telling of them – her favorite was the way the tree smelled. Something she could have done with her eyes closed. It was his turn to look down and smile at the innocence.

"It reminds me of something my dad told me when I was younger. I was questioning Santa's existence." Harris looked at Harlow as she laughed at the serious way he'd explained his life-altering moment. "I had argued and researched – always the worker, always trying to move forward."

Harris thought of the reason he was there with her tonight, enjoying rather than dutifully executing, but for a business venture nonetheless.

He continued. "There was no possible way one man, even with the help of magic – which I strangely didn't seem to have a problem with – could deliver all of those presents in one night. And stop to drink milk and eat cookies on top of it."

Harlow laughed at the young Harris' reasoning, impressed by the thought and detail.

"After all, nobody could eat *that* many cookies and not feel sick, which would also inhibit Santa's ability to continue." Harris nudged Harlow with his elbow to get her to smile a bit wider.

"Anyway," he went on, "my dad sat me down and told me Santa is as real as I want him to be. Because he's not something you see, he's something you believe in. So, I closed my eyes, and rather than see, I tried to feel."

Harris broke eye contact and looked up at the tree. "I swear in that moment I heard laughter from my family in the kitchen, Christmas trumpets playing music, and silver bells chiming where we hung them outside. I felt more in that moment than I ever had, so without seeing him, I knew he was there. I knew that Santa was real, and always would be."

He hadn't thought about that memory in years. The simplicity of the moment – like the scent of pine.

"I love that. It's perfect," Harlow said, loving the vulnerability of the recollection. She wondered if there was a fun-loving, sentimental kid, rummaging around beneath Harris' sleek black façade? She hoped she'd get to see it over the next couple of days. Assuming he'd stick around for all of the Christmas wish events. She'd written a hefty list.

"What do you think of this one?" Harlow asked as she looked from the tree to Harris, hopeful, because she loved everything about it.

Harris skipped playfully as he began his assessment and started to move around the huge base.

"Well," he began, stealing a look behind him to see if she was following, "it has a nice trunk and a straight spine – critical for a space that will be viewing the tree from every angle. It seems, if you have at least a million ornaments, the branches are sturdy yet the needles are surprisingly not deadly to the touch." Harris used his pointer to prick the end of a needle, and Harlow chuckled and nodded agreeably.

"It seems it's the perfect shade of wintery green with," he leaned in and sniffed twice, "just the right amount of piney smell." He leaned back and nodded, "Yes, I think it might be just right, except…"

Harlow's head swung around and she looked at him. "Except? Except what?"

"I don't see the ladder."

"The ladder?" Harlow asked, confused.

"A tree this tall should definitely come with a ladder," Harris said, decidedly.

"Ha-ha." Harlow faked a laugh through the genuine one that bubbled up. Then smiled slyly, "We *have* a ladder. And that's what you are for."

She skipped away before he could ask if she was serious, then he looked up at the tree he'd almost commented was too tall, but decided she'd probably had taller.

"What I'm for. Right," Harris said to himself, and looked down, resigned.

Well, he thought, if he died or seriously injured himself decorating a tree the size of Paul Bunyan, at least it would be a good story. And he'd be in the presence of the most mesmerizing and enchanting woman he'd ever met.

And better yet, the sooner they got decorating the sooner he could schedule that strategy meeting. Maybe it was worth the risk after all.

CHAPTER 11

Harris had thought the house was impressive when he'd arrived earlier that evening. Then, the light from the sun had still been shining, and shadows cast from the trees danced lightly over the exquisite façade. But now, as they turned into the curved drive, he didn't have words to describe the enchanting view now that day had turned to night.

Snow-covered lanterns burned like fire, flickering in the dark. The crystal chandelier that hung from the wooden dome in the entrance looked like a captured star exploding rainbow reflections on the walls and through the windows to be seen from the outside. Lights from the halls of the house gave off a distant amber glow that could be seen from the bedroom windows that lined the front of the house.

"It's amazing, isn't it?" Harlow asked, her simple words filled with sincerity.

"I've never seen anything quite like it." Harris admitted. He had passed the homes on Summit many times. He lived next to impressive brick houses in his gated community – success and hard work had given him that.

But this? This was something different. It was all of the beauty of the past – *Christmases past*, he thought grinning to himself – standing tall and immaculate in Christmas present.

"I feel that way every single time I come home. I have to pinch myself a little bit. Even having grown up with this house, *in* this house, I still can't believe it." Harlow looked at Harris when he'd slowed and came to a stop.

"Well, are you ready?" she asked.

Harris looked up, his eyes climbing the stone steps, and took a deep breath. When they'd asked if he wanted the tree nursery staff to put the base on the two trees they were able to take home with them, he'd refused, wanting to be macho. The only reason he'd given in was due to Harlow's insistence it's how her family had done it for years. Now he was thankful all they had to do was struggle to get it up the stairs. And, he thought, one of them up multiple flights of stairs. Maybe he could talk her out of the bedroom idea, but he guessed probably not.

At that thought he watched Harlow cheer and jump out of the car with the enthusiasm of a child. *Here we go.* Harris pushed his door open and joined her on the outside wondering just how to get these things down.

—

An hour and two breaks later, they had the trees set up. One in the great room, and one, because 'of course it has to be up there,' in Harlow's bedroom.

Harlow looked at the grandfather clock sitting in the living room where they plopped after retreating to the couch, both offering loud huffs as they made impact with the large pouf cushions. When they heard their simultaneous reactions, they couldn't control their exhausted laughs.

Harlow noticed it was after eight. She'd been enjoying herself, actually having fun, with a man she no longer considered a complete stranger. But she didn't want to wear him out on the first day. That is, if he even intended on coming back.

"It's getting late." She moved her head to the side so she could see his profile. It was a good profile. A wide, strong, square face, with a straight-line profile. "You're welcome to dinner, but I don't want to keep you."

Harris shifted his head so they were face-to-face. "Dinner sounds great, but I should probably get going."

The pang of disappointment hung in her chest and she wondered if he was already finding a place in her heart. That was where she felt the feeling coming from, wasn't it?

"I have a pretty busy week, but I'm free Friday. They'll have the tree delivered by then. If you're free, we can decorate?" he asked with a grin.

Harlow smiled as she recalled her second Christmas wish. She wouldn't have suggested it herself out of pride. And not wanting to request his services when, in this one night, he'd already done so much.

But since he offered, and she longed for it, she couldn't refuse.

"Friday sounds wonderful," she confirmed, and watched him push away from the couch. He did a turn in the living room and shook his head again in disbelief. She felt proud of his reaction. Not boastful, not from superiority, but because of the hard work she'd known had contributed to building this house – this home. And she learned, in people's disbelief, was appreciation.

Harlow fell into step behind Harris as they navigated to the door. She grabbed his jacket and hat from the iron coat tree while he slid on his shoes. When he reached for the handle, she didn't know what to say so she just said, "Thank you."

Harris smiled genuinely and thought how strange it was that this beautiful woman, in this huge house, could be standing there thanking him. But in the short hours he'd spent with her, he was starting to understand. She wanted to be surrounded by people. Needed the same magical feeling of love she so fondly remembered as a child. And, he realized, she was stirring something in him as well.

And for that, he agreed. "Thank you, too."

CHAPTER 12

Harlow curled her hair in long carrot-red waves, wore a green plaid print dress, and donned her red toggle coat to match her red lips. She skipped into the office and only stopped humming *Rudolph the Red-Nosed Reindeer* to laugh at herself for splashing her gingerbread latte out of her cup.

She continued her tune straight through the office, pausing only to wish Sally, Jacquelyn, Ryan, Vanessa, and Lisa a Merry Christmas as she floated by each desk. She halted briefly when she crossed the threshold of her office to mimic Santa in a deep jolly tone.

"Rudolph with your nose so bright, won't you *guide my sleigh tonight?"*

The audience exchanged bright-eyed, amused looks, then shooed Lisa into the office with waves of their hands, and a pointer-finger from Ryan, that just said *go!*

Lisa skirted around her desk and nearly got hit in the face with the red stocking cap that flew toward the hook next to the door.

"Okay," Lisa laughed, "What has gotten into you?"

"Why, whatever do you mean?" Harlow smiled sweetly and quietly started her humming again.

"Oh my God, you're turning into that crazy Christmas lady from *The Nutcracker*. You can't cope, so you're freaking out and faking happiness. Before you know it, you're going to turn all of us into toys and take over the seven kingdoms." Lisa looked up, wondering if she'd gotten the movie reference right in her sleepless stupor.

"Her name is the Sugar Plum Fairy, and I'm *not* turning into her. Nor am I attempting a takeover of the *four realms*." Harlow's eyes danced with laughter at her friend. "But, I am taking over," Harlow looked up and started using her fingers to count the rooms as she imagined walking through her home, "six, twelve, thirteen, fourteen," her words sounded small, "fifteen…sixteen rooms of The Hill!"

"I think a takeover isn't necessary seeing as you already live there, yes?" Lisa asked, amused and enjoying her friends' excitement, and casually wondering if she'd gotten the *seven kingdoms* from *Lord of the Rings* or one of the other epic fantasies Steve made her watch with him this time of the year. In-home movies were the closest thing they could get to date night these days.

Harlow finished a sip of her latte, crossed her legs, and leaned in, "I am taking them over and filling them with Christmas magic!" She threw her arms up and cheered, then brought them down and added, "Or, I will be, Friday. When Harris comes back to help me. In the meantime, I'll try and haul as many boxes up from the basement as I can."

"Whoa, whoa, whoa. No, no. You can't move onto boxes. Did you just say, 'When Harris comes back?' Like, Harris was there already? Helped you? And with what? And is Harris *a man?*" Lisa finished then got up, circled the chair she was sitting in, and dragged it closer to Harlow's desk.

When Lisa sat back down, she placed her notepad and coffee on the desk and waited. She crossed her legs and held her knee to indicate the patience she would have, and that she'd wait – and not move – until she was given something.

"Okay." Harlow broke.

It was one word, and at it, both of the girls leaned in and hovered over the desk for a much needed, delicious round of gossip.

Harlow explained everything from the embarrassing postbox run-in, to finding her Christmas magic resolve, and Harris adorably showing up at her door with a wreath, and embarking on a Christmas tree shopping extravaganza.

"He stuck with you through all of it?" Lisa asked, not believing anybody could have embodied the patience it would have taken to shop for something as important as a Christmas tree with Harlow – much less three. She'd need to meet this guy.

"He did. He was sweet, gave advice, let me lead, offered to get hot chocolate and mini donuts – though by that time we were both starving and hadn't eaten since lunch. But he made it. He told me this sweet story about him and his dad and believing in Santa Claus." Harlow felt her face go dreamy but she couldn't help it, even though she knew it would lead to what Lisa would ask next.

"You like him."

Harlow noted it wasn't a question, but a determination. She thought about it for a minute then nodded, slowly at first.

"I like him. He was very nice, respectful, kind of funny, and you can tell he loves The Hill. That gets me, you know? When they have a soft spot," Harlow admitted and Lisa nodded.

Yes, Lisa thought, she knew, and grinned.

"Well, are you going to tell me what he looks like?" Lisa finally asked since Harlow hadn't offered.

"Imagine a young Brad Pitt mixed with your favorite hockey player. Handsome, cute, square, and sturdy."

Lisa cracked up, "Did you just say 'square?'"

"Yes!" Harlow copied Lisa's laugh but defended herself, "Like a nice, boxy rectangle. Ha! That's so much worse," she exclaimed. "He's skinny but he doesn't look like a beanpole. I know you know what I'm trying to say."

"I do, but it's just so fun letting you try and explain it," Lisa admitted with an innocent smile. "Wait, Christmas tree shopping." Lisa couldn't believe she hadn't put it together. *"He* answered your Christmas letter?"

"I have my very own, Christmas-wish-fulfiller-man, provided graciously by what I can only assume, was Santa."

CHAPTER 13

One snowfall, five event site visits, thirty boxes (until she stopped counting), and one berry-colored poinsettia delivered Thursday afternoon with a card that read:

> *To add to the magic.*
> *See you tomorrow.*
> *Always,*
> *Harris Porter, Christmas wish aficionado and extraordinaire*

Now it was Friday, and she still couldn't keep the smile from rounding her freckled, blushed cheeks at the thought.

Harlow had made an excuse to move her final Friday afternoon meeting to Monday so she could head home and make sure everything was in place for when Harris arrived. Or at least that's what she'd told herself.

Harlow ran out of her bathroom with wet hair spraying behind her. She paused only to sniff the tree they'd hauled up a week earlier, then she grabbed the robe off her bed, swung it on, and ran back into the bathroom to dry her hair. Her finger tapped her phone screen to check the time and to click the volume up so Michael Bublé could be heard over the blowing of her dryer.

As the blood rushed to her head from flipping it upside-down to finish the drying she wondered if Harris would stay for dinner. If he would want to order in, or embark on the adventure of cooking together.

She stood up and flicked the dryer off. Harlow wondered if it would be strange, navigating the kitchen with another person. A man.

Her last boyfriend, Andrew, always insisted on going to his place. Harlow hadn't admitted it then, but she'd hated it there. It wasn't the size of the St. Paul apartment she didn't like, it was how cold and impersonal it felt when she was there. There weren't pictures, art, or any sense of home. And his kitchen had made the meal that ended up marking the end of their relationship – thank God.

Was it weird, then, that she wanted to make dinner with Harris? Something about him seemed good and sincere. A little uptight, and clearly wanted to carry a certain image.

What was it? she thought. Was it importance? Success? Class? It seemed natural and forced all at the same time.

Maybe while they made dinner she'd have to learn a little more about her Christmas wish-granter extraordinaire.

It was decided then, they'd make dinner. It was her Christmas wish after all.

—

The tree looked magnificent in the foyer. Harris tried to think of the right word but none of the others seemed to do it justice.

"It's good, right?" Harlow asked, as she held her hands in front of her, nervous that her excitement was a little too much.

"Good? It's unbelievable. I can't believe how perfect it looks in here. Amazing. Magnificent," he decided, nodding in her direction and grinning at the little bounce she did while fiddling with her fingers. She really did love this, he thought.

"It is. You're right. Magnificent." Harlow agreed. "Are you ready to get started? Oh, and how do you feel about dinner? Have you eaten?"

"Dinner sounds great. Should we get started then break when we feel we are too famished to go on?" Harris asked.

"Yes! But we can't hardly decorate a tree without refreshments."

"No truer words have ever been spoken. What have you got?" Harris cringed at his question. "I should have brought something. I didn't even think about it."

"You mailed me poinsettia Christmas magic yesterday, I think you're covered for tonight."

"Fair enough – and I'll take what I can," Harris agreed, and found that he liked that she liked the poinsettia.

He had found himself unable to leave it behind when he saw the bright red leaves. Everything about it – the vibrant way the petals mixed their reds together on the table, the playful way they bounced as people shuffled in and out of the isles and grazed them as they walked by – it reminded him of her.

He was finding she was on his mind more and more. Harris was sure it was just the silliness of the season. And if that was the case, why not just let her linger there for the time being. Besides, it had made him a bit happier, and made him enjoy everything just a bit more.

———

They had climbed up and down the ladder, strung bright white and amber colored lights. More strings of lights than he had put on any tree in his lifetime – combined.

But he had to admit, when they'd turned it on, it had the desired effect. He was getting excited to put the ornaments on. When he started moving toward the boxes that had *ORNAMENTS* written on the sides in giant letters, her voice had him stopping.

"As much as I consider wine a meal, and it has been on multiple occasions – more than I'm willing to admit – I think I might require real food. Are you feeling like you could eat?" Harlow asked as she peeked out from around the other side of the tree, talking loud enough to be heard over the speakers that were allowing a holiday mix of oldies and new goodies to be heard throughout the house.

Harris paused long enough to realize he was really hungry. He glanced at his watch and saw it was almost seven. He mirrored her peeking motion around the tree and said, "I am more than feeling like I could eat. What's for dinner?"

"Whatever we want. Let's go look." Harlow stepped into view and held out a hand so she could lead him toward the kitchen.

When he took her outstretched hand, Harris was glad she'd excitedly turned away to lead them through the dining room toward what he would describe as the butler's pantry, and into the kitchen.

Instead, he felt how her hand seemed so comfortable in his. He tried to push it away and tell himself it was innocent, and that it wasn't the first time she'd dragged him behind her. Hadn't she done the same thing the first time they'd met? So why now, after he'd spent more time with her, after it shouldn't be strange, was it that he was feeling affected by their touching? The realization that he was overanalyzing their hands followed his eyes in a roll back to reality.

The first thing he noticed in the kitchen was a never-ending line of upper and lower Cherrywood cabinets, and an island that spanned the length of the room. Three enormous, sparkling chandeliers hung over the island.

Just some of your run-of-the-mill pendant lighting, he thought, as he shook his head at his internal sarcasm, smiling in spite of himself.

"Okay, we have pasta with endless sauce possibilities. We could have breakfast. Or–" Harlow trailed off, her mouth starting to water at the idea of pancakes or French toast but she was cut off.

"Did you say breakfast?" Harris asked, intrigued at the mention.

"I might have."

"Like crispy bacon, sausage, eggs, and hash browns?" Harris walked toward her until they were face-to-face.

Harlow arched a brow with intrigue and nodded slowly as she worked her way through his list. "Yes," she admitted, not having thought about the wonderful savory additions, "all of those, as long as we can make pancakes or French toast as the perfect sweet accompaniment."

Harris bent his knees slightly and leaned back while saying, "Mm, I haven't had French toast in years. It's a deal. Breakfast for dinner."

"Breakfast for dinner!" Harlow's voice matched her skip to the fridge, and she heard Harris clap his hands and rub them together – a sure sign he was ready to get down to business.

How great to have gotten somebody like him to fulfill her Christmas wishes. He was making it so fun. And, she thought as she scoured the fridge for eggs, milk, and cream, he was the most handsome man she'd ever spent the holidays with. All two days they'd spent together – so far.

"What are those?"

Harlow watched a flare of concern flash across Harris's face at the question.

"*They* are eggs, milk, and cream." She couldn't help the smile.

"What do we need those for?" Harris asked, genuinely concerned at what he'd signed up for.

"The French toast. How did you make the French toast the last time you had it?"

"The toaster?" Harris asked rather than stated. As if asking if that was an acceptable way to make French toast.

Harlow laughed and nodded. "Though extremely efficient, I think what we'll have tonight will be slightly better. Dare I say it, you might never again crave a freezer French toast."

"If that's a challenge, I accept." Harris bowed in acceptance, rolled up his sleeves, and moved toward her, ready for his first assignment.

The pearly island top appeared yellow where the egg mixture had spilled and splattered out of the bowl while they whisked. Grease droplets speckled the enormous double gas range from the salty bacon. And the otherwise smooth counter surface was rough to the touch with breadcrumbs from slicing thick cuts of ciabatta before they were left to soak.

Run Run Rudolph let out a blare of rock and roll and Harris couldn't help but do his best impersonation of his dad rocking and flying fingers across a fake piano.

Harlow squealed out an excited laugh at the sight and joined in, pausing only to freeze and belt out the catchy tune, then they danced around like fools while tending to the fragrant meal.

Harris waited for Harlow to finish flipping a caramelly looking toast before grabbing her hand and whirling her around in a mixture of spins and twists. He pulled her close, swung her out, then lifted their arms over their heads and slid out until their hands caught them before they fell away.

Laughter was the only interruption to their words straight through the song. On the final note, Harris pulled Harlow close and dipped her low. Harlow's head fell back as she tried to catch her breath through the joy and heartbeats pumping through her body.

When she lifted her head, their eyes met and they smiled. Their laugh turned to chuckles as the moment captured them, unable to move, enraptured in a stare.

"You've got nice moves, Harris Porter." Harlow smirked and wondered if Harris realized just how much fun he was having. She hoped as much as she was. "I wonder if I might ask where they came from?"

Harris grinned at the question as joyful memories found their way in once more. "My dad," he started, while moving the bacon from the sizzling pan to a paper towel-covered plate, "I suppose, both mom and dad, when they used to dance. Not just around Christmas, but I remember it more vividly at that time. Dad refused to let us get sucked into the commercial side of Christmas and forced us to do things as a family."

Harlow sneaked a glance in his direction, wanting to see his face. Did it bother him, the family time, or was he remembering it fondly? Because even as he said those first couple of words she found herself longing for a moment like that.

"At the time I rolled my eyes." Harris looked at her, catching Harlow in her studying gaze. "But now, as I remember or think about those moments, it makes me happy. Back then I'd think my dad was such a dork, but after a minute I'd forget all about it and we'd all be joining in, mom and dad, my sisters and me." He let out a breathy laugh and said, "I like getting to do that again, it's been a long time."

The admission wasn't hard, but the realization at just how long it had been tugged at his heart. He wasn't blind to see Harlow was the one bringing it out of him, either. Her crazy Christmas wish was bringing a flood of memories back, and he was finding he hadn't realized he was missing them.

Just then, without thinking and while standing side-by-side over the stove, Harris leaned over and kissed Harlow on the cheek, lingering just enough to let it warm and to see her close her eyes and lean into it just a bit.

CHAPTER 14

They ate on the floor of living room, sitting around the piles of food they'd set on the square coffee table. *Elf* played on the television in the background but they'd hardly watched a minute of it.

"Who would have thought." Harris let his mind work with the sweet sensations in his mouth from the last bite of French toast. "Cream, vanilla, syrup, and cinnamon – all to make French toast. A damn good French toast."

"I'm glad you like it. You were a very fine kitchen assistant," Harlow agreed professionally, pretending like she remembered more than just the kiss he'd placed on her cheek.

It had only been two days, but she already knew she was going to miss him when he was gone. So, she wouldn't think about it and just enjoy.

"'Like it' might be a vast understatement. It's the best I've ever had. And assistant?" Harris covered his heart as if wounded and joked, "I cooked that bacon all by myself."

"I stand corrected," Harlow agreed. "Executive, kitchen assistant."

"I'll hold the title proudly." Harris sat up a bit straighter accepting the title and the pride that came along with it. "So, do we start with the ornaments?" he asked while he stacked plates to take back to the kitchen.

Harlow did the same and let the squish of the pillow she'd been sitting on bounce her up and down, then stood and agreed, "Ornaments! Then the rest of the room. Then," Harlow moved her finger to the right, "the other rooms."

Harris nodded and stated his thoughts out loud, "We are going to need more than one day. We are going to need a weekend decorating extravaganza."

Harlow didn't want to get her hopes up, but the idea made her giddy. She even hoped for more snow. Not enough to hinder travel from Harris' house to hers, but enough to make it beautiful to add to the wonder the weekend would bring – if he was being serious.

"Are you sure?" she asked as they set plates in the sink. "I don't want to over-Christmas you in one weekend. There were a lot of things on that list. And really, if you feel like it gets to be too much, I get it. This is a lot to ask of somebody. And you've already made it so fun."

"I'll let you know when my wonder wears out. Until then, if you don't have any plans, I think we have a winter-filled weekend ahead of us."

"If you're sure…"

"As sure as I am that I know the real Santa Claus." Harris paused, then continued at her questioning stare. "I know the real Santa Claus," he confirmed, then walked back through the pantry and the dining room, where she'd taken him to enter the kitchen, and found the foyer.

Harlow watched him navigate the floorplan like a man on a decorating mission. How cute was this guy? Santa really knows how to pick 'em.

She saw Harris heave a box off of a stack and onto the floor to dig in, then covered the giggle with her hand when she heard him yell as if she'd been across the house to ensure she heard him.

"C'mon! Let's get some music rollin' and work up an appetite for hot chocolate!" Then, before the music could begin, he started to sing his own version of *Blue Christmas* and turned to put the first ornament on the tree.

CHAPTER 15

Harris walked into work Monday humming the same *Blue Christmas* song he'd let linger in his head throughout the weekend. He did a quick little tap-dance to stomp off his soggy shoes a couple times on the mat then shuffled his feet in tune to his hum.

Nancy watched the show from her perch then started clapping in applause accompanied by a hoot and holler.

"You're a regular Elvis." Her quick laughs came out as crisp as the weather.

"I'll be here all week." Harris gave a bow and shared in her amusement. He'd known Nancy too long to be embarrassed that she'd caught him, and even then he didn't really know if he cared.

"Merry Christmas!" Santa cheered as he walked into the building behind Harris.

"Merry Christmas!" the two said in unison.

"By the look of you both, I missed something fun. I do enjoy everything fun." Santa stopped and let his belly wiggle like jelly as he Ho-Ho'd. "I have more letters for you, Mrs.

Nancy. It's a full one today. Seems we had another great weekend."

Harris thought to his own weekend and grinned while agreeing with Santa, "It seems we did."

Though his thoughts drifted to a certain red-head with porcelain skin. And to the way her skin didn't so much blush, but kind of glowed as it warmed. He'd seen it after he'd kissed her cheek in the kitchen. The idea had him thinking about spending more than just the holidays with Harlow.

Harris wondered if he had the time for both work and an amazing woman. He'd never had to worry about that before – never wanted to. Or, rather, never let anything get far enough to.

He was making sure their family created wealth and that generations after him could benefit from it. That people would know their name. That his father and the fathers before him, the risks they took, and the poor life they endured wouldn't happen to their family ever again.

The stories his dad had told him and his sisters when they were young brought a healthy respect for work, and for him, the incurable drive for more – more business, more profit, more money. And, he thought, the more they made, the more they could give.

"Harris," Santa started and rested a hand on his shoulder, "your father tells me you've enlisted your services in a Christmas letter of your own. It seems it's going well?"

Harris cleared his throat wondering if Santa had been reading his mind. "It is. It's going very well. I'd-" Harris paused at the words he was about to say, but they fell out because he wasn't able to find more that could replace them, "well, it's been a long time since I've stopped to enjoy certain moments of the Christmas season."

His words were genuine. More than once Harlow had encouraged the joy and excitement he'd felt as a child around Christmas, and he'd brought those thoughts – and more – home with him at night.

He'd even stopped to get his own tree. It didn't have any ornaments, but he'd strung bright green and white lights all around it and kept it on all night so he could wake up to the glow of them. Just as he had when he was a boy.

"It's a good thing you're doing. I have a good feeling about this. I believe when you help one, you end up helping many. It seems giving has a sort of ripple effect," Santa said and looked over to Nancy when she agreed whole-heartedly with what he was saying.

"Well, I better be on my way. Lots of Santa duties this time of year."

Santa walked away humming the tune to *Blue Christmas,* and had Nancy and Harris looking after him wondering if he had heard them just moments before, or if it was pure coincidence he'd picked the same melody for his own that day.

"He'll never stop amazing me," Nancy said. "And, neither will you." She eyed Harris.

"What do you mean?" he asked absently, wondering what he did that she thought was amazing. It took a lot to impress the likes of Nancy Lawson.

"Usually you're all business. Walk in, dutiful hello's, then straight up to work. This is a side of you I don't know if

I've ever seen. Don't start thinking about it. You've always been perfectly wonderful, this is just," Nancy thought, not usually one to have to search for words, "brighter." Nancy beamed to match her word.

"Brighter." Harris bobbed his head back and forth as if contemplating the adjective. He thought it seemed like a description he would have given Harlow and smiled at the thought. Yeah, he'd take it. "I like it. It seems bright is a good thing to be around the holidays, don't you think?"

He asked the question as he came around to place a sweet kiss on her cheek. At the way Nancy reddened and giggled unexpectedly, he decided in that moment he would appreciate her just a bit more. He always had, but now he'd make more of an effort to show it.

—

The ambition and drive to work hadn't lost its edge amidst all of the holiday fluff. It seemed the energy he'd found in the season was lending well to the amount of work Harris had to get done in the office.

He and Brandon had met earlier that morning. In the one week he'd given Brandon to start moving forward with the collaboration, he'd identified budget resources, a tentative schedule that would go through a round of approvals, and the different farms and businesses that would potentially benefit from the collaboration.

This could really help a lot of people, he thought as he spun his chair around and took in the St. Paul skyline. To the normal eye the overcast haze would have seemed gray and gloomy, but to his it was silver and prepping for dusting of snow.

"I don't know if I've ever seen your chair facing that direction." Charles Porter walked into the room as Harris smirked and turned his chair back around, "You're usually face-down in something more important than what's going on out there."

"I think snow is very important at this time of year," Harris said, wondering if that was a line he'd ever thought, much less said out loud. He figured most Minnesotans might disagree – or agree for a little while, but adamantly disagree when an April blizzard swept across the state burying any hope of spring.

Charles eyed his son while nodding. He didn't want to comment that Harris had never paid attention to the weather or its effect on the holidays before. But he wouldn't say it out loud.

"How's everything going?" Charles wondered if they'd made progress on the collaboration and, if he admitted it, was a little surprised he wasn't briefed on it already that morning. He wasn't in a hurry, but usually his son would have had something on the calendar before he could even sit down and enjoy the last bit of his coffee.

"It's great – better than great," Harris confirmed. "It's been fun to get to spend time with Harlow. We've put up trees, decorated them, decorated the house. When we've needed a break we've cooked meals to Christmas music and had hot chocolate. I'm pleasantly surprised at how this assignment has played out. This coming weekend we are ice skating with a couple of her friends." Harris looked at his dad sideways and wondered aloud, "I can't remember the last time I've been ice skating..."

Charles stared at Harris with one side of his lip twisted up in amusement. It took him a couple seconds to shift gears and follow along. He had been expecting an update on the collaboration, and Harris was giving him a recount of the Christmas letter he'd been answering.

"I suppose it was after the hockey game in Duluth. Do you remember that?"

Harris' question shocked his dad. Charles had no idea Harris had remembered that. He was old enough to remember, of course, but it was such a simple thing.

Harris' hockey game had ended – a tough loss to a strong Hermantown team – and everybody seemed worn out and a little down. Barb had suggested they all go for hot chocolate before the trip back to the cities.

The hot chocolate they'd found was in a little hut next to a pretty ice-skating rink set up for the holidays. Charles had parked and they all looked at each other wondering if it was too much effort. But Kayla and Ashley, Harris' sisters, had sat through endless games that weekend and were ready to do something that didn't require more sitting. They bounded out of the car and left the others no choice but to follow.

Charles smiled at the way Harris had grumbled about having to move, his muscles exhausted.

"I think every inch of my body hurt after those games." Harris smiled, keeping up with his fathers' memory of the night.

"I didn't think you'd get out, and I wouldn't have blamed you. Played damn good that weekend," Charles added to make sure Harris didn't think the skating was all he remembered.

"Kayl and Ash ran right by the chocolate and asked that poor stand attendant for free skates." Harris laughed and shook his head. "I can't believe that kid caved."

Charles's laugh was big at the forgotten detail. "They did that, that's right. And," Charles looked at Harris now, "I think you saw how much fun your sisters were having and didn't want to take the moment away, so you joined in."

"You heard them cracking up, nothing would have – or could have – stopped that." Harris tried to avoid the admittance, though he had always had a soft spot for his sisters. They were always there. In the stands, on the sidelines, no matter how far they had to go – they were always there cheering him on.

"You three got that whole rink to join you in a game of skating tag. Even those little kids, they couldn't have been over five. The parents stood on the side laughing and cheering."

"*Then* we got the hot chocolate," Harris said, thinking of how much his side had joined the rest of his aching body, only that particular pain was from laughing too much.

"Everybody sat in a big circle on the ice and drank together. What a moment." Charles admitted, looking down and shaking his head, trying to pull every detail into his memory. Then he smiled and he saw Harris smile back and made a mental note to add this moment to his long list of favorite memories.

—

Brandon walked in when both of the men were sharing more stories from Christmases past. The way they'd stopped talking at his greeting caught him a little off guard and had him stumbling to a stop and holding a stare in their direction.

"Brandon, come on in. I wondered if I'd catch you both," Charles said as he waved Brandon to the chair next to his own. "What do you have so far?"

Brandon looked to Harris, wondering if he should take the lead or let Harris run the recap. When Harris gave a friendly nod, Brandon smiled and began walking the two through the details of the collaboration. Charles had asked some questions but overall, they'd covered a lot of ground in the short time they'd been working this.

Charles sat and took in all of the information. The timing, he thought, would be all up to Harris. He wondered…

"I like it. Now there's the question of timing. What are your thoughts?" Charles directed the question to Harris. He told himself he wouldn't mind the *when* – as whenever it happened to be it would be great for both companies – but he'd be lying if a little part of him didn't hope Harris would take the holidays to slow down.

Harris paused and thought on it. He thought about his schedule with Harlow, and all the things they had planned. And, of course, the actual holidays that were Christmas and the New Year.

It left him two full weeks of work in December – he was counting out the week of Christmas for any type of productive activity. Then twelve weeks would take him to the second quarter. They could do twelve weeks. It would be tough, but they could do it.

"What about Q2?" Harris asked Brandon directly, but looked to both of the men for input. If he wasn't mistaken, Harris thought he saw a flicker of disappointment flash across his dad's face before he lifted his eyebrows and turned to Brandon for the actual timing. Nobody had to do math when Brandon was around.

"Sixty-six working days if you don't count the week of Christmas or New Year's," Brandon confirmed and went on without prompting. "We can do it in sixty if nothing goes wrong and we don't miss a day. *If* Pro Feed agrees to the collaboration schedule."

Harris' excitement was growing as they discussed the details. He could feel the energy pulse through his body, and nodded his head.

"Yes," Harris said, first to himself, then to the others. "Yes, let's do it. Dad, any objections? Aside from making sure I'm home for Christmas?"

Charles let out a breathy laugh at his son's exuberance. He might as well accept and be glad that Harris liked the family business. It could have been worse.

"Okay, let's go for it. Let me know what you need from me in the meantime."

The three men stood up smiling. Harris and Brandon's smiles were big, boyish, and giddy at the new challenge they were about to take on – with only opportunity laying before them. And Charles, though slightly less so as he tried to hide a wish his son would slow down, joined in. Then they all shook hands at their new venture and went on with their days.

Charles paused once in the doorway to look back at the two younger men who were already hovering over Brandon's laptop.

Though he wouldn't wish for his and their families' lives to have been any different, he wished just a little that his son would know their world wouldn't stop turning if he let a little Christmas magic of his own come over him. He wished Harris would slow down just as the year did when winter fell upon it.

He might just see there was a little more wonder out in the world with family and friends than in here working toward a number.

When he heard the men laugh, Charles smiled and closed the door behind him. He walked back to his office to call Barb and tell her he loved her and wish her a Merry Christmas, like he'd done as a young man when he'd been trying to woo her over a holiday of their own.

CHAPTER 16

Lisa and Ryan watched Harlow practically burn streaks into her office rug with the pacing she'd been doing. She was going to contemplate the pros and cons of inviting Harris to the hockey event Friday right through her floor.

"It's in two days," Harlow started again and turned at the end of a pacing line, "that's not enough notice to give somebody for something like this. And," she added, making another turn and rounding her eyes with the words, "it's an *event like this.*"

Lisa smirked toward Ryan, who was getting far too much enjoyment out of his boss's anxiety over the man that was quickly becoming a regular mention in her friend's casual conversations.

"Can you explain to me a little bit more what exactly *'event like this'* means and why it's important here?" Lisa asked through a yawn, "Sorry, not you. You're not boring. Baby. It's the baby."

Harlow nodded her understanding in passing. "Public. Very public. Lots of people, people he'll meet, they'll wonder..."

"Wonder about what exactly?"

This question managed to stop Harlow. When she looked up her face brightened like a lightbulb. A realization had come to her.

"Lisa. Exactly, exactly."

"Sorry, now you lost me," Lisa said, shaking her head and looking to Ryan to see if he was following along. When Ryan shook his head, they stared absently in Harlow's direction and waited.

"You guys, *wonder about what?* Exactly! *What?* Because there is no *what.* Don't you see? I can't believe I even worked myself up so much. It won't matter because we – Harris and I – aren't anything."

Harlow held her hands out to indicate there was nothing in them, using charades to aid in her determination. "Nothing at all. He's just a simple Christmas wish deliverer and I am a gracious wish accepter. Nothing more, nothing less. Besides, it's a holiday charity event, it's super Christmassy. It makes total sense that this would be something he would tag along to."

Harlow placed her hands on her hips to watch the understanding slowly come to Lisa and Ryan's faces. Their disbelieving nods were in slow motion, but gaining strength the longer she stared – and the more narrow Harlow made her eyes.

"Yes," Ryan said when he looked at Lisa, who had clearly not been trying to indicate there was nothing going on between the two seemingly perfect pair, "you're exactly right." Ryan confirmed shooting Lisa a look that said *help me out a little here.* "So, just go ahead and call him, tell him you have a great charity event at the rink Friday and you think he'd enjoy it. You could even say 'it might be fun.'"

The cheesy smile Ryan gave was missed by Harlow but didn't slip past Lisa as she caught on to what he was doing.

Harlow's finger bounced up and down at his logic and she ended with an unmoving point in his direction. "You know, yes, I think I'll do just that."

She whirled around her desk and pulled out her cell phone and scrolled to: *Harris Christmas Extraordinaire,* then clicked his name with her thumb.

"Harris, hi, it's Harlow," Harlow said and smiled to Lisa and Ryan as she heard his response. Then she mouthed *he knew it was me.*

Lisa pinched her lips together to hide the humor behind them that was trying to escape, and heard Ryan whisper to her, "She knows he can see who's calling, right?"

"Let's just let it be," Lisa said, tapping Ryan's shoulder, encouraging him to drop it and let Harlow have her moment.

"It's a charity event and I thought you might like it," Harlow continued her conversation. "You would? Oh, that's great!" Harlow did a little dance in the room and wasn't ashamed. Besides, she would have done the same had it been anybody else on the call, or so she told herself.

"I'm excited. Sure, my house at four-thirty?" Harlow said, then stopped and held her breath. "Okay, yes, sounds great. See you then." Harlow listened to Harris' sign off and lost the little color her porcelain skin had and her mouth gaped open.

Lisa stood first but Ryan beat her in their movement toward Harlow. They'd seen her change in an instant.

"Harlow, are you okay, what happened?" Ryan asked, genuine concern wrenched out with his words.

"He said, 'it's a date' then hung up." Harlow said with a hint of fear in her own words.

Ryan barely held in a snort and Lisa craned her neck so Harlow couldn't see her silent laughter. Lisa rubbed Harlow's back and said, "Oh, I'm sure he didn't mean it. You two will still go as friends. It's just a figure of speech. Don't worry about it at all."

Harlow straightened and grabbed the mug from her desk and left the two in the office alone.

"It's totally a date." Ryan said.

"Yes, but she doesn't have to know that."

CHAPTER 17

The clothes that were piled in the middle of Harlow's bed looked like a mountain she could have skied down. Every outfit she tried on became a fresh snowfall to the top helping it grow.

Casual. People would be casual there, she thought. But she needed to look cute. But she also *didn't* need to look cute. No, she thought, she *wanted* to look cute – for herself. Or, that's what she decided to tell herself.

Harlow marched to the side of the mound where she'd tossed the discarded sweaters, pulled out a camel colored turtleneck sweater, and held it up. She took a turn on a point and decidedly marched right to the leopard booties with a nice sturdy heel. Then raised her head high and picked up the black skinny jeans – the same jeans she'd had on two pairs ago and had decided against.

Warm and cute, and the ankle boots were just a bit sexy.

"See, that wasn't so hard, was it?" Harlow asked herself when she changed and turned herself in front of the intricate, antique floor mirror.

When she turned back to look at the mountain she sighed and thought, okay, maybe just a little hard. Then she started laying shirts and jeans flat, one on top of the other so she could easily slide the hangers in and haul them back into her closet.

Just as she was putting the last of the jeans away Harlow's phone began to ring and the sound of *Jingle Bells* filled the room.

"Hello," Harlow smiled and sang into the phone after accepting the call.

"Hi, are you ready for your *casual night out?*" Lisa asked with a baby offering cooing noises in the background.

Harlow's heart fluttered at the sound and went mushy on the inside. She had *almost* missed the way Lisa had described the night she was about to go on, but caught it and loved her more for it.

"*Yes,*" she said proudly, looking at her now-clean room and the outfit she hadn't wavered from once. Okay, maybe once, but hadn't changed out of when the act of putting the clothes away forced her to go through her entire closet for a second time. "I am ready, looking super wintery, and I am going to be nothing but relaxed and excited. Because," Harlow took each step down the stairs deliberately as if she were making a point, "this is just a friendly and fun night out."

Harlow slipped off a step as she tried to quickly halt herself when she saw Harris' SUV pull into the curve of her driveway.

"Lisa!" Harlow whispered. "He's here!"

Lisa's smile reached through the phone as she said, "You'll have a blast. And I'll let you go so you can say hi and get on your way."

"No, wait," Harlow whispered again.

"Why are you whispering?" Lisa asked, still amused.

"I'm spying on him from the fourth floor. He just pulled in." She gasped and forgot her need for quiet, "He's getting out. Oh, gosh dang it!" Harlow stomped her foot on the marble step, causing an echo from her chunky heel.

"What? What is it?" Lisa asked.

"He looks so cute. No," she corrected, "he looks *handsome* today. No, no, no. He's not supposed to look handsome tonight."

"I would ask what he's wearing but I fear that would only make it worse for you. Instead I'll try logic." Lisa paused and made sure she had full attention. "Do you think there's any possibility that he looks handsome tonight, because, well, he is in fact…handsome?"

"Hmm." Harlow considered the question. "On any other day I'd give you that one. But today he has on a black sweater with super cute jeans, so no, not at all. Tonight, he's *super* handsome. You know people with blonde hair look good in black. Like the kind of good that looks better than everybody else? It's a *thing.*"

"Then here's what I think," Lisa started, "I think you know that you are just as good looking as he is. So rather than worry about how great looking *he* is, when you're out there tonight just know that everybody is going to wonder who that beautiful woman is who's with him."

"I can be beautiful today," Harlow said, agreeing with Lisa. Or, trying to convince her mind to stop spinning at the sight of Harris because it was making her dizzy and letting the rotation reach her belly.

"Yes. You are beautiful. Every single day," Lisa added, "but especially today. And I should remind you, you are also fun, witty, and charismatic – all of which add to your beauty."

"Lisa," Harlow said, firm and resounding, "you're right. And, I'm going to holly the jolly right out of this holiday charity night."

"That's my girl."

"Okay, he's at the door, I'll talk to you tomorrow and let you know how it went."

"Sounds good, have a great time."

"Thanks, talk to you later."

As soon as the friends hung up, the doorbell rang.

—

The charity event was sporty and masculine, and Christmassy and wonderful. The perfect combination of casual and classy – the environment was casual, the cause was more than classy.

All of the funds raised that evening were going to the Children's Hospital – every last penny. Even the work Ryan had done putting the entire event together with his team was pro bono. Harlow had seen to that detail, but agreed to give Ryan all of the resources he'd need to pull off an event like this. And, as Harlow turned circles in the middle of the rink, she saw that he did.

Pride, Harlow decided, was what was coursing through her. And, she added to herself, all of the cheerful beauty of the holiday that surrounded her. And maybe a little bit of hope.

She and Harris had met some of the kids that were patients at the hospital shortly after they'd arrived, and each one of them had stolen their hearts.

So now, she hoped. She hoped with everything inside of her that this night would help with the care they needed, and would give them a Christmas like every other happy child would have that year.

"Your company put all of this together?" Harris asked as they stood back-to-back looking around at the winter spectacle.

"*Ryan* did this. Ryan and his team. They nailed it," Harlow admitted leaning her head back slightly to talk over her shoulder. "He needs a raise," she acknowledged, knowing Ryan had surpassed her expectations and deserved serious recognition.

"I don't know much about event planning but I'd say 'nailed it' could possibly be an understatement." Harris looked up and watched the trees on every level light up to the beat of the Christmas music.

"You nailed it." Harlow grinned.

—

Harlow had seen Ryan in passing a couple times and noted he seemed to have everything under control. She also noted that Harris had known and introduced her to just as many people as she had to him.

She'd overheard him talking about everything from pee wee hockey to high school grudge matches. It was a side of him she found fun, exciting, and just the right amount of competitive. The amount that made him not only handsome, but sexy. Even though she didn't care about that or think about it while with a friend on a casual night out.

Harlow stood a bit straighter and offered a hand and a greeting to one of Harris' childhood friends – who also happened to be a forward on Minnesota's professional hockey team.

"Mr. Randall, it's so nice to meet you," Harlow greeted the hockey player who had an uncanny resemblance to Paul Bunyan with his massive beard and matching body.

"Please, call me Zane. It's nice to meet you, too." Zane gripped Harlow's entire hand in his own and shook. "This is the best event I've been a part of at this rink. What a turnout. But then, I'd turn out for this display any day."

Harlow tried not to stare at the hole where the missing tooth should have been in Zane's grin and smiled back at him. "Thank you for saying that. It really means a lot."

"So, speaking of charity," Zane shifted his weight and sent his question to Harris, "how are the letters going this year? I'd love to help again if I can."

"They are really pouring in. I am still amazed at the amount we get in. Most of them make me smile. Some of them still make me wish we could do more." Harris smiled and added a shrug knowing they could only do so much.

"Count me in for gifts and I'll do another trip this year – for who's ever asking for one." Zane nodded, understanding too well having to balance income with giving. But when it came to kids in need, he never wavered. That's why he'd come out tonight.

"Thanks, Zane. I'll touch base next week to see what we have and give you the details."

Harlow had followed the conversation and it didn't take her long to realize they were talking about the same letters that had been mixed with hers. Letters from kids wishing for things they really needed. Or, she thought, hoping for something they could only dream about, and relying on the magic of Christmas to come through for them. And there she had been, not having a want in the world, and selfishly asking to re-live already wonderful childhood memories with her own letter.

She'd do something about that, she thought, the next time she could get Harris alone.

Maybe she could turn her Christmas wishes into something that could be shared. After all, she'd have the time, seeing as she'd be solo for the holidays. The thought nearly made her roll her eyes but she decided she was too happy to let the Christmas blues sneak in.

When it was time to gather on the rink for the opening ceremonies Harlow and Harris made their way through the crowd and joined Ryan, other charity staff who helped put on the event, and members from the Children's hospital.

A massive velvet green bow wrapped the center of the ice where they stood and took pictures after charity and event organizers spoke and thanked everybody for coming out for such a wonderful cause.

Harlow had only teared up twice as she listened to stories of kids miraculously recovering and of how some of those kids who had since grown up, were some of the most generous when it came to giving back during the holidays.

The head of the charity told her own story of being given the gift of Christmas when her own prognosis as a child hadn't had her living beyond her twelfth year. She believed the generosity of caring donations had aided in her recovery. Medicine and miraculous health care for sure, but the giving spirit of others and the magic Christmas had lent to her healing.

When Harlow had tried to hide a stray tear, Harris had gently circled an arm around her to comfort. Rather than the lust she'd felt earlier, a tenderness had taken over and she worried soon she wouldn't be able to trick herself out of liking Harris Porter.

More pictures were taken and hands had grasped in greetings and introductions. New clients were added to their prestigious and growing list. And holiday cranberry martinis were sipped and enjoyed.

"Harlow." Harris had walked toward her from a group he'd been talking to a few feet away. His smile melted her heart as his eyes grew with excitement, "Can I steal you away for a minute? There's somebody I'd love for you to meet."

Harlow smiled at the doctors she'd just met and graciously excused herself, then said, "Of course, is it Santa Claus? Because I already know him."

Harris' laugh reached his belly and thought, something close to that. "He's a close second."

They made their way over and Harris began the introduction.

"Calvin Crane. I'd like for you to meet Harlow Hill. She's-"

"Hill?" Calvin couldn't help himself and cut Harris off, "Of the St. Paul Hills? You've got the house on Summit?"

"Mr. Crane, it's very nice to meet you. I would be one of those Hills. Hopefully that's a good thing," Harlow said, looking to Harris with an intrigued eyebrow and got a small shrug in return.

Harris continued with the introduction when Calvin Crane simply laughed at what he assumed was her joke. "Calvin is the COO of Pro Feed, a company we will be working very closely with over the next couple of months – hopefully longer."

"We hope the same thing," Calvin added. "It's really great to meet you, Ms. Hill." Calvin nodded excitedly. "Our family is from up north and would travel down to St. Paul every year for a Christmas weekend. We'd do a play, great restaurants, and drive around and see the lights. We always drove down Summit and especially loved *The Hill* – your house. How lovely to meet you in person."

Harlow had been skeptical at first, wondering who this crazy man was, but after hearing his reasoning, a soft spot began to form. If he loved her house, it almost automatically made her love a little bit of the crazy in him.

"Thank you for saying that. It's really nice to be a part of such a fun memory of yours," Harlow said, but changed the subject, hoping to get it off of her, "What type of work will you be collaborating on?" She looked from Harris to Calvin.

"Hopefully something that will help farmers embrace technology a bit more when it comes to feed, storage, and distribution," Harris said. "It really could be a huge benefit to both of our companies. It's in the early stages," Harris looked to Calvin to show comradery, "but I think if we push hard, straight through the holidays, we'll make really good progress."

Calvin's enthusiastic nod was hard to watch and not laugh at. Harlow tried her best to cover her humor with a wide smile and matching nod. If you can't beat 'em, join 'em, she thought.

It was enough to get Harris to hide a laugh in a fake cough behind his drink. The action only made him laugh harder and earn a concerned pat on his back from Calvin. But the concern only reached his gesture, as he was completely on board with the timing.

"Absolutely," Calvin confirmed, "we have a team working day and night with Brandon – he works with Harris – to ensure we don't lose a single day in December. We even have some people working on Christmas Day."

The comment halted the amusement, though she'd tried to hide it. "Wow, really?" Harlow hoped the question would keep him talking but she only received another nod.

If that was the case, she thought, the time she had with Harris wouldn't be much, and it would definitely end before Christmas.

The sadness swept through her quickly and she could only stare and try for a pleasant smile to hide her true feelings.

Which, she realized, was that she wasn't ready to say goodbye to Harris.

In fact, she admitted, not knowing if it was the man or the magic of the holidays, she found herself falling head over skates.

CHAPTER 18

Winter, Harlow decided, was giving her the perfect amount of glittery snow to carry out her Christmas wish-list with Harris in snow-globe fashion.

They'd skated in circles, twirling, racing, and gliding to an overhead speaker that gave an old crackly record feel to the music as it billowed out over the park. When Harris had challenged a young boy to see who could reach the end first, Harlow had caught up to them, announcing the young boy victorious, and they laughed so hard they both fell over the made-up finish line.

When Harris grabbed Lisa's husband, Steve, for a beer, the two girls made their own figured cuts into the ice and gossiped about work, and as women do, their men.

"So, you and Harris seem adorable together," Lisa said, transitioning from a conversation about Sally and Ryan and how they both wished the two would admit their feelings for one another. Their logic was simple – they were too cute not to be together.

"I don't recall a question in there. Was that a statement, or are you fishing?" Harlow asked with a smirk and linked her arm through Lisa's so they could skate in sync, side-by-side.

Lisa held tight to Harlow's arm and grinned her response. "I am simply stating the obvious and leaving the floor – or rink – open for comment." Lisa paused but only for a second. "Because come on, if you can't see how cute you two are together, you're blind. And I've seen the way he's been sneaking looks at you. Skating close to you and finding excuses to take your hand. Frankly, it's adorable."

"Coming from you, I'm going to take that as a compliment – seeing as you and Steve are the adorable champions." Harlow was amused at her friends' candid observations.

"We have a baby now. All the *adorable* we have is letting the other sleep through one of their middle-of-the-night two-hour shifts." Lisa's look was serious. "And let me tell you, the words, 'It's okay honey, I'll take this round, you sleep' is the sexiest thing Steve's ever said to me."

Harlow laughed at the description of the two parents to precious Layla, and wondered if they realized what a miracle they had made. The beautiful family they had become.

"You, all three of you," Harlow said, "are darling. And you're amazing parents."

"Well, thank you. When I wake up from sleep skating I'll appreciate your words all over again. But seriously, have you thought at all about telling Harris how you feel?"

The two rounded another curve and Harlow smiled as Harris came into view and returned his wave from the perch at an outdoor bar-top table the men had taken.

For a moment she simply stared and let the wonderland slow around her, and really look.

Harris was in jeans and a sweater for their night out. He was casual and not dressed to impress that night. Yet somehow, he was more attractive to her than any of the other times they'd been together.

Harlow watched his easy smile, and a glance in Steve's direction acknowledging and laughing at something Steve had said, but not taking his eyes off her.

Their time together might have been to check things off a list, but the memories he'd shared with her, the dancing and the laughter they'd had together, she hoped he knew just how much the time had meant to her.

He'd become more to her than somebody that was answering wishes she'd scribbled on a sheet of paper. He was becoming the person she wanted to text during her day at work when something was funny. Who she wanted to call at night while making dinner alone and wishing he was there to cook with her. He, she admitted, was someone she missed having in her home when he wasn't there.

Harlow looked at Lisa now and her smile didn't fade, just fell a little. "I can't tell him how I feel. Because I know he wants things in his life right now that don't include me. He needs time to focus on work, and I'm looking for somebody that's willing to put work aside and spend time at home. Somebody who would be willing to take the entire month of

December off, not who would work straight through Christmas day."

Lisa listened and they glided in silence until she nodded, and carefully said, "I understand, but I think you should give him the chance to decide that for himself. It is the season for miracles after all."

When the four had skated until their feet were numb from the cold, and laughed until their sides hurt, they finally traded their skates in for the warmth of their boots. As they rounded the rink and exited through a wooden gate toward the firepits that circled the rink, they greeted and thanked a group who was just leaving and offering them their warm and crackling fire.

Harris lowered himself onto a stump, slid another right next to his, and pulled Harlow down next to him and pulled her close to keep her warm.

"Ice skating." Harris made a big check mark in the air with his free hand. "Check another off the list."

Harlow threw up her hands and cheered, "Yes!" Then held her hand high while Harris smacked hers for a gloved high-five.

"You two are making me look bad." Steve joked as he scooted two of the stumpy logs over so he and Lisa could join them. "Cut me some slack over here, huh? We have a baby at home, it's hard to be magical on three hours of sleep."

"Oh, that's so cute and romantic." Harlow sighed at Steve's words, ignoring the fact that he probably felt like a zombie. "You two are embarking on the ultimate romance. Relying on each other when you're dead tired, loving sweet

Layla when she needs you, and you still like each other. *That's* hard to do on three hours."

The group laughed but how Harlow had described their friends' romance caught Harris by surprise. He didn't expect something so innocent, and clearly meant to get a laugh, to rock him like it did.

But the idea that two people went through so much together, the type of love they shared when they truly cared for the other person, it really was powerful. He'd never thought of it in just that way, but now, images of his parents and their lives growing up had him seeing his own parents differently.

They'd done that for him and his sisters, given them all of their love. And for the first time in as long as he could remember, he thought, the memories they'd made as a family had nothing to do with money or the growing success of the family business, and had everything to do with his parents love.

Harris felt himself pull Harlow a little closer. He held on a little tighter to the woman who had asked for simple Christmas wishes, but instead had given him the greatest gift he hadn't known he was missing — love.

CHAPTER 19

The night sky had cleared as the snow fluttered its last flake and left stars glistening in the sky like a reflection of the snow-covered ground below. Even with the temperature dropping, Harlow and Harris couldn't bring themselves to part with the night.

Their logic was simple: they were already freezing and couldn't feel their fingers and toes, so they might as well enjoy the night a little bit longer before heading in to warm themselves by the fire.

They walked under the lamplights next to magnificent homes that, when lit up, could probably be seen from outer space.

"Lisa and Steve are pretty great," Harris said, grinning while mentioning Harlow's friends. "If you're into that perfect-couple, romantic-comedy thing."

Harlow's laugh sang out and it was music to Harris' ears.

"I don't know that anybody has ever described them more accurately. They really are obnoxiously cute, aren't they?"

"Beyond irritating," Harris agreed, exaggerating his joke, but feeling as if he'd been friends with them for years.

They fell silent and Harris spoke again. "It's refreshing."

"Out here?" Harlow asked, wondering if it was a bad time to tell Harris she might need new toes by the end of the night. And noted the two pairs of socks she'd donned under her boots, favoring practicality over vanity, was one of the best decisions she'd ever made.

"That too, but I mean Lisa and Steve. It's refreshing to see two people together who just seem to believe in each other. They have fun, yeah," Harris shrugged, "but they don't sugarcoat the hard stuff. They accept it, laugh at it, and work their way through it. Their midnight wake-up routine is comical when hearing them joke about it, but I bet at night when they are both dog-tired it's not very funny. But here they are, still in love, still doing it."

Harris looked at Harlow and stopped their momentum. "I like everything about it."

Harlow looked at Harris and decided his eyes were more hazel than brown as she searched his face for any sign that he might kiss her rather than look for more words. She closed her eyes and leaned into his gloved hand as it gently moved a stray red curl away from her face, tucking it just under the brim of her stocking cap. His hand lingered on her cheek as he slowly moved toward her.

"Harris!"

The two jumped at the sound of Harris' name.

The startle and quick embarrassment of being caught in the intimate moment had them pulling apart just far enough to prove they hadn't been doing anything wrong.

When they looked out to the shops on Grand they couldn't help their grins as they watched Santa happily march toward them waving like only the jolly man could.

"Santa, it's great to see you. I didn't think we'd have company out-and-about with us on a chilly night like this." Harris slid a glance and a grin in Harlow's direction and loved the red that blushed her face.

"Oh, you know me, at this time of year I'm everywhere. There's so much that needs to be done." Santa winked at Harlow and offered his bright round cheeks in a smile. "How are you doing young lady? I'm happy to be able to see you out and about again."

"I'm doing wonderfully, thank *you*, Santa," Harlow said, hoping this Santa was real enough to read her mind and know she was thankful he'd sent Harris to fulfill her Christmas wishes.

Santa winked and she couldn't believe the warm feeling that came over her as she heard him say *you're welcome*. Only he hadn't said it out loud, but she'd heard his voice clear as day in her mind.

"Harris," Santa continued, "I wonder if you wouldn't take a few of these letters I just pulled out of the postbox and bring them to Nancy on Monday? I have an appointment in the morning that I can't miss, but I don't want these letters to be delayed because of me. Would you do that for me?"

Harris perked, "I would love to, not a problem at all. I hope your appointment isn't anything serious."

Santa leaned in close as if he were about to tell a well-kept secret and said, "Nothing a little Christmas magic can't handle." Then he leaned back and held his belly in a *Ho-Ho* that seemed to light up the whole man.

Harlow and Harris stood bewildered at what they were witnessing and wouldn't have known how to put it into words if they tried. They half expected Rudolph to fly down and pick Santa up so he could be on his way.

"Well, thank you both so much. I just love running into people while I'm out and about. It seems it is never completely coincidence. I find we come across people exactly when we need them. I'll be off," Santa added with a glance toward the letters, leaving little room for their reply. Though, as they stared after him, they weren't sure they would have had much more to offer than their "Good bye" and "Good night" anyway.

—

The great room warmed quickly as the fire sparked to life. Harris had forgotten the satisfaction of a simple small flame flickering into a wood-burning blaze.

He sat back on his heels, took it in, and nearly moaned out the satisfaction he felt from the warmth melting away the cold chill from his body. When he heard the sound of glasses rattling on a silver tray he turned to see Harlow walking in with two crystal stemmed glasses and a matching bowl filled with creamy-gold liquid.

Harlow saw the wonder slide across Harris' face and offered, "Eggnog. Are you for or against the 'nog?'"

Harris smiled and gave a casual nod in response. "I am for the 'nog." He stood and moved to her, helping her with the tray and setting it on the coffee table. "Though I don't remember buying it in a crystal bowl. Ours mostly came in glass or plastic bottles and we'd store it on the deck outside in the snow."

"In the snow, great idea."

"You say great, I say lazy. The kitchen was farther away than the deck, but in our defense, one can only step away from *Christmas Vacation* for so long without fear of missing something you hadn't seen the first fifty times you watched it that year."

"I think that makes it all the more brilliant. But this," Harlow used a ladle to scoop the smooth light yellow liquid into the glasses and said, "is homemade. My grandmothers' recipe. I haven't met a single person – that likes eggnog – that hasn't agreed this is the best they've ever had. Are you willing to try it? I should warn you, I don't think there's any going back after this."

"In that case," Harris took the glass she offered and clinked his to hers, "to never going back."

Harlow sipped and watched his face light up in delighted surprise. She couldn't help the proud feeling that filled her up as she recognized the familiar reaction. It happened to everybody who had ever taken a sip.

"Well?" she asked, wanting to hear his thoughts.

"I can never go back," Harris confirmed. "I'm finding myself wanting to drink the whole thing, but fighting that urge so I can enjoy every drop. What a wonderful battle to have to play with oneself."

Harlow laughed and agreed. She'd never quite heard it explained in that way but she understood exactly what he meant.

"I think you've hit it on the 'nog.'" She grinned and tried not to laugh at her cheesy joke. Then her eyes moved to the table where Harris had set the letters. They were calling to her and tugging at her heart, wanting her to read them.

"I know it's not my business, or my company, but if you wouldn't mind I would love a chance to read some of the letters. To see what people are asking for – what they need."

Harris couldn't say no to her genuine tone, so he took her hand and led her to the pillows next to the fire and helped her down. They leaned back against two tall chairs with fabric seats and elaborately carved wooden frames and matching legs, and opened each card one by one.

—

They'd read all twelve letters, then sat quietly as the fire crackled and hissed offering warmth and comfort. A warmth and comfort, they realized, these twelve kids didn't have.

It seemed Heritage House – the same orphanage Vanessa's event was supporting – had let their young children write letters to Santa and dropped them off earlier that day.

Harlow let a tear slide down her cheek and Harris reached over and wiped it away.

"This is why we help," he said gently, trying to comfort but feeling a sadness inside himself that matched hers. "So they don't have to feel so alone at Christmas."

"What you do is wonderful." Harlow tilted her head and looked at Harris when she saw the lines of his face crease and fall into a frown.

He didn't want to admit to Harlow he'd been too focused on work to pay attention to the letters that had flooded in over the past few weeks. He'd been worried about a collaboration and growing their business. He hadn't given more than her Christmas letter a thought – and *that* had been forced upon him by his dad. He would have never voluntarily taken on the task. Not for her, or any of these letters.

Harris shook his head, a silent gesture telling her he was fine. And he was. He was more than fine. And he was able. He'd do something about this.

Both of their heads turned at the knock on the door. Harlow and Harris stood and moved to the door together. When it opened they stared at Santa holding another letter in his hands.

"Santa?" they both questioned in unison.

"Sorry to barge in on you like this, but it seems I'd forgotten a letter to hand over. I'm hoping I can trust you with this one, too." Santa moved his hand forward so the letter hung between them.

"Of course," Harlow said as Harris took the envelope. "Of course. This, and any more you have, we can take. We'll be sure they get to the right place."

Santa's smile spread so wide his round cheeks forced his eyes into happy slits.

"Thank you both. Now, I do think I'll be able to leave you to it for the rest of the night."

Santa turned and stopped before the first step and looked up, "This is a beautiful home. I bet the warmest holiday parties have been hosted here. What a magical experience people must have had when they've come. I do love a great Christmas party."

Then he turned and was off. Harlow and Harris stared after Santa for the second time that night. When they finally turned themselves and closed the door behind them they stood where they were and opened the letter.

Dear Santa,

I'm already thankful for my mom, dad, Bert (he's our dog), and my brother, Maximillian (but we call him Max). I'll get a lot of presents this year, so I don't need anything. I'm hoping maybe instead you can add my Christmas wish to my friend's so he can have two.

My friend said he asked for a teddy bear to sleep with at night because sometimes he gets scared. That can be his wish. Maybe you can use his second wish to find him a nice family. I know it doesn't work that fast so while you work on that it would be really nice if he could have a nice Christmas with lots of food and presents. I don't think he gets all of that at his big house.

Oh I almost forgot, his name is Mikey Andrews. He's at the really big house with all of the other kids.

Thank you, Santa.

Taylor Brink

Harlow couldn't believe what she'd just read.

"Harris!" She ran to the great room and shuffled frantically through all of the letters until she found one and held it up. "Look!"

When Harris realized what she was holding his face lit up.

"Taylor's friend is Mikey from the orphanage." She read through his letter one more time and saw the sweet way he'd asked for a teddy bear that wasn't too big, but wasn't too small either. And thought of Taylor's request.

If he could have a nice Christmas with lots of food and presents.

"That's it!" Harlow popped up and was in front of Harris so quickly he nearly moved to avoid a collision. "Let's have a Christmas party."

"A Christmas party sounds great." Harris agreed and tried to keep up with Harlow's enthusiasm. "I'm sure we could find a place that could let us in last-"

"No," Harlow said quietly, calming herself and Harris, and lifted her hand to his chest and shook her head, "no, let's have it here. I want to open this house up and share it with those precious kids. Let's give them the best Christmas they've ever had."

Harris grinned and stared at Harlow. She'd done it again. She was amazing. And he was the one lucky enough to have fallen in love with her. With everything about her.

"Yes, the absolute best they've ever had," Harris agreed and pulled Harlow into him and he held her in a hug that meant more than any other embrace he'd ever given.

CHAPTER 20

Harlow opened her eyes the next morning to a stream of light shining through the curtains of the great room, and the sound of a sizzling fire that had burned throughout the night keeping them warm. Her hip was sore from the position she'd slept in, nestled in the crook of Harris' arm and chest, but she didn't want to move.

As she looked at their leaning bodies she realized they'd fallen asleep with papers and lists all around them. She smiled at the excited way they'd begun their Christmas party planning the instant they'd had the idea. It was going to be spectacular.

Speaking of spectacular, she thought, coffee would be a close second to snuggling with the handsome man she had fallen for.

Harlow moved the papers away from their laps without making a sound and slowly eased herself from the couch so she wouldn't wake Harris. She covered him with the a stitched, red and cream holiday quilt, and moved to the kitchen to start a strong pot of coffee.

Harlow lingered over the pot, resting her hip on the side of the countertop as the hot water gurgled through the rich espresso beans, and she thought about the days to come.

There were a lot of logistics, but she figured her team wouldn't mind some extracurricular holiday planning. Ryan was working on a New Year's Eve event, but the others would have the time. And she wouldn't be surprised if Ryan still found time to chip in where he could.

Harlow shivered at the chill that had filled the house over the winter night. She hugged herself for warmth, but also reveled in the feeling. She knew some people didn't like the cold, but to her it was simply another reason to seek out a warm sweater, flannel pajamas, fuzzy slippers, and a fluffy blanket that would comfort while sipping a warm drink.

She even liked that the winter darkness brought late mornings and early nights. To her, the night stretching farther into daylight only allowed for more time to enjoy the festive lights that lit up the city and neighborhoods.

When the coffee finished brewing, Harlow filled two thick mugs, and returned to the great room. As she entered, she found Harris giving the fire another log. Not too much, but just enough to take the edge off of the morning chill.

She couldn't help the love that welled up inside of her when he turned and offered her a caring smile with his mess of hair and a small wave.

Harris motioned to the fire and said, "I figured we could warm up a little before we head out. Thanks." Harris took the offered mug and sipped. "Nothing better than that."

"Definitely." Harlow thought, agreeing mostly with herself that there wasn't anything better than the feeling of love that had just swept over her.

"Did you just say 'head out?'" Harlow asked when she'd stopped daydreaming long enough to process his comment.

"I did."

"Where are we heading to?" Harlow grinned at his coyness, then took another sip.

"We, as they say, are going to get two bluebirds with one stone."

"Bluebirds, very nice."

"I thought so," Harris said, agreeing his holiday addition to the saying had a pleasing seasonal ring to it. "We," he continued, "are going to check off a Christmas wish *and* do a little Christmas party prep."

"I think I love the sound of that."

"But are you ready for it? That's the question." Harris glanced toward Harlow who was sitting next to him with her feet beneath her.

Harlow's look of question showed a hint of concern. "I need to be ready?"

"It's Christmas cookie day."

"I *love* Christmas cookies!" Harlow exclaimed while bobbing up and down on the cushion. Her excitement caused them both to lift their steaming mugs to keep the hot coffee from spilling over. Harris laughed at her response.

"Not a lot of people get excited about meeting the family. Your reaction is…refreshing."

"Your family?" Harlow asked, choking a bit as she tried to finish a gulp.

After he got the reaction he was looking for he grinned and added, "Don't worry, they aren't that bad. Their standards are only *near* perfection when it comes to Christmas cookie baking. I'm sure you'll do fine."

Harlow processed his words while images of the day to come raced through her head. She imagined standing next to Harris' mom while trying to impress his family with her baking prowess. Somehow, in her thoughts, she ended up making a fool of herself while practically begging them to love her.

Harris kissed the side of her forehead as he watched the barrage of facial expressions match the nervous look on her face. He didn't do it to be mean; it was a lighthearted joke. But he'd be lying if he didn't say he wasn't taking in a little bit of joy in her reaction.

Because, if he was assessing her correctly, she was worried because she wanted his family to like her. And, if she was worried about them liking her, *she* must like him.

"I'll be down here while you get ready. No rush. Cookies start at ten."

"Ten!" Harlow sprang from her spot on the couch, "That's only two hours from now!" She turned and left him alone as she gave herself a pep talk on her way out. "Shower, hair up so there's no chance of it falling in cookies. Something cute but wearable for standing and baking all day."

Harris chuckled at the sound of mumbling that drifted away she made on her way to the stairs. He stole another glance as he watched her reroute and turn toward the kitchen.

He couldn't see her but he could hear added mumbles of needing more coffee and the clink the pot made as she placed it back into the machine. He caught a glimpse of her as she passed through the hall and found the bottom of the stairs and made her way up.

This, he thought, could be his life. It was, he realized, the life he didn't know he wanted but couldn't keep out of his mind. Waking up next to Harlow, lazy mornings together, nights out with friends and a morning event with family.

It was the first weekend in years he wasn't taking one, or both, of the days to work. It had taken him his whole life to appreciate it, but Harlow had thrust him into it. For that, he would forever be grateful.

—

The ride to Harris' mom and dad's house was the quietest she'd had ever been. Harlow found herself trying to find casual conversation but kept getting lost in her thoughts with every new comment or question she tried to conjure.

What if they hated her or thought she was pretentious? Or if they'd pictured Harris bringing somebody home that was completely different than her? But that was ridiculous, she thought, right?

Because really it was just as he'd said, they were checking another item off her Christmas wish list. So really, he wasn't bringing her home to meet anybody. He was bringing a spoiled woman home to bake cookies with his family because she'd asked for something so silly in her letter.

When they pulled up to a beautiful old house in a nearby St. Paul neighborhood, all Harlow could say was, "Your parent's house is not nearly far enough away."

Harris laughed at her nerves and comment, then reassured, "I'm sure they will love you. Just trust me," he added, noting he didn't know a single person his family didn't like. And if you added the fact that he was bringing a woman home for the first time ever, they'd probably start doting on her the moment she walked through the door.

Harlow and Harris reached the front door, and rather than knock he turned the knob and walked right in.

"Don't you think we should knock?" Harlow asked, worried they were barging in.

"At my own childhood home? Not a chance. Besides, if I can scare my mom and sisters, the break-in is worth it."

It was enough to get her to smile and shake her head at the mischief in his eyes as she followed him down a hallway toward the back of the charming home.

The inside, she noted, was just as inviting as the outside. When they'd pulled up she'd taken in the two-story brick house with black shutters. It was decorated with green garland, big red ribbons, and colorful lights. The inside was the same traditional style but with all of the feelings a warm home could bring.

The scent of cinnamon greeted them, and pictures of family memories smiled back at her in a collage of heavy frames that lined the hall as they walked. She slowed to linger over Harris as a young boy and lifted her hand to her heart when she saw the bright-eyed, innocent boy with his arms draped around two adorable girls who must have been his sisters. A hint of longing for her own brother and sister bubbled up but she pushed it down just as quickly.

Harris took her hand and asked if she was okay.

As Harlow nodded, she whispered, "Everything about this house is wonderful."

He squeezed their intertwined fingers and led her toward the light and laughter emanating from the kitchen.

"Merry Christmas!" Harris said in a cheerful greeting as he walked through the opening.

Harlow watched his mom and sisters jump at the startling surprise, and double over in laughter as they turned. His sisters shoved at his shoulders before wrapping him into a squeeze so tight it seemed as though they hadn't seen him in years.

Harlow laughed at the sight and glanced over to see Harris' mom offering the prettiest smile before she opened her arms and moved toward her.

"Harlow!" Harris' mom beamed with delight, then circled her arms around Harlow and simply held. "We are so happy you could join us today. I just can't tell you all of the wonderful emotions I have swirling inside of me."

Harlow felt Harris' mom twirl her finger against her back demonstrating her emotions, and she couldn't help but return the embrace.

"Thank you so much for having me. I can't remember the last time I spent the day making cookies."

Just as she was about to let go, she felt his sisters join the hug and listened to them greet her in the same friendly manner.

Harris looked at his dad and rolled his eyes at the love circus occurring before them, then dropped his head and shook it. "How come I don't get *that* when I come home?" he said, directing his question to Charles, who was sitting at the kitchen table with a newspaper scattered in front of him.

Charles leaned back, peered over his glasses, and nodded. He was holding onto the joy that filled his heart at his son who had finally come home to spend a simple – but special – day with the family. Charles offered his feelings with a grin and a comment: "It's good to see you, too, Harris."

Then he winked and motioned for Harris to join him at the table, and slid a thermos of coffee toward him. "Might as well sit. These women look like they might need a minute."

—

Eight hours, one nap, and a mountain of cookies later, Harlow, Barbara, Kayla, and Ashley fell onto the couches in the living room that sat off of the kitchen, and all let out an exhausted puff of breath. They'd baked every cookie Harlow could have imagined and more.

Sugar cookie cut-outs, chocolate crinkles, ginger cookies, sparkly spritz, Russian tea cakes, peanut butter blossoms, thumbprints, and mint swirls. There were more she'd already forgotten, but she'd felt so accomplished when the last batch came out of the oven and the last of the dishes were cleaned.

Harris walked in from the deck with a fresh beer and a plate full of steaks from the grill that were covered in foil to rest before dinner.

Only in Minnesota, Harlow thought, would a family grill in the middle of winter. She supposed it's why so many kept brooms and shovels tilted on the outdoor railings all year long. So they could shovel and dust their path to drinks and dining.

"I don't know why you all look so tired. It's just baking." Harris feigned simplicity in the work. He expected griping in return, as he'd only helped for a couple batches somewhere in the middle of the day, and his back ached just from that. But what he got instead were pillows to the face from every direction.

Charles laughed from behind and asked, "Harris, when are you going to learn? You have to dote on the hard work that's been done in the kitchen, because then they'll let you try some of their handiwork."

Charles eyed the sugar cookies – his favorite – then slid a glance toward his wife for approval. Upon a nod from the love of his life – his Barb – he snuck one that had slightly browned edges, then drifted to the front of the house to enjoy it.

When Ashley and Kayla sprang to their feet to finish tormenting their brother, Barbara got up and walked across the living room to join Harlow on the couch. She sat slowly but only so she could get close and cherish the intimacy of this new special woman in Harris' life.

A woman who, for the first time since Harris was old enough to make his own decisions, had come home to bake cookies with his family.

Barb lifted Harlow's arm and slid hers beneath, linking them before resting them once more.

"How are you doing after the long day Harlow, dear?" Barb asked, smiling toward Harlow.

Harlow turned the up corners of her lips and tried to stop her emotions from tipping over. She moved her head back and forth as she tried to find a way to express how thankful and grateful she was to get to share the day with such a wonderful family.

"Oh honey, it's okay. It was so great to have you with us." Barb soothed as Harlow wiped away a tear.

The two didn't notice the commotion from Harris and his sisters had stopped. When the siblings saw the embrace in the living room they each grabbed their own cookie and moved to the front to join their dad, leaving their mom alone to work her magic.

"I'm so sorry. It's so foolish to cry after what is now going to be my favorite day of the year." Harlow said, and laughed while her sweater sleeve cleared more of the tears.

"It's not foolish at all. It just makes me feel like you understand what a simple day like today means. But I wanted to tell you, it means so much more to me."

Harlow looked at Barb who, like her, had glossy eyes.

"For a very long time Harris has been the hard worker of the family." Barb nodded, agreeing with herself. "We tried to limit what the kids could have growing up, knowing that so many went without. I'm afraid rather than the lesson we were trying to teach, Harris felt the need to help our family be successful instead of accepting the wonderful things we already had. But this time, seeing him today, I see a shift in him. Do you know this is the first time I've seen him not pick up his phone to work one time? And it's the first time since he's moved out that he's been here to make cookies."

Barb waited for Harlow to laugh and went on.

"I know your family name," Barb admitted. "I'm sure many people do. It's hard for people to see through the money. We've done well but live humbly, and people still only see the money. They see a house and cars. They see what they think is success."

Harlow waited it out, wondering where Barb was going.

"Not many people see that a house isn't a home until it's shared with the people we love. That beautiful things, though we can cherish them and love them – as I know I have many things I've been handed down through generations that I adore – it never replaces the feeling of family. Of love."

Harlow looked at her hand which was looped with the hand of one of the kindest women she'd ever met, and nodded. Barbara, in such a short amount of time, had understood.

"Harlow, dear, you have brought my son back to me. Whatever it is that you have done to him, I hope he realizes the wonderful love you've shared with him and have for him."

Harlow's head shot up. "I-uh, love? No," she looked away, "it's just…" She paused, giving in, "it's only me."

Harlow sat for a minute, then finally admitted, "I love *him*. It's not the other way around. He's such a wonderful man, but we want different things. I want what you're talking about – a house filled with a family. And Harris? Well, I think Harris wants to succeed. And he will. Because he's so driven and responsible. He's wonderful."

Barb swaddled Harlow in a hug and gently placed a motherly kiss on her forehead and thought, this sweet girl will know soon enough she's captured the heart of her only son.

CHAPTER 21

Harlow's heeled ankle boots clacked across the floor as she swung through the narrow path bordered by desks that led to her office. Her bag and her never-ending Christmas party lists dangled off one arm while her coffee marched back and forth with the exaggerated swing of the other.

"Up, up, up!" Harlow said as she speed-walked through her office door. "In here! All of you!"

Harlow smiled without looking back as she heard the shuffling of papers, and chairs screeching as they shoved away from desks. She heard a thud, a skid, and a grunt as one of them collided with their desk, and winced knowing she'd caused the hurry.

Lisa was the first through the door wondering if she should be amused or panicked. Then Sally, Ryan, Vanessa, and Jacquelyn piled in, one so close to the other, they looked like a single being with four heads.

Harlow threw her deep, forest green jacket on the back of her chair and stood in a fitted red sweater and a plaid skirt.

It was the most professional, Christmassy outfit she could find that morning, and she'd wanted to set the right mood.

It was Day One of official party planning and they only had five days. It had to be this Saturday, or none at all. Christmas Eve was a week from tomorrow so this was their only shot. She needed all hands on deck.

Harlow looked at her staff, took a sip of her gingerbread latte, and got down to business.

"We need to pull off a minor Christmas miracle. It will be hard." She let her stern face fall to pieces and grinned. "But it's going to be *so* much fun. And I want you all to work together. Then we all take the entire week of Christmas off. Except for Ryan – sorry Ryan." Harlow scrunched her nose acknowledging that Ryan wouldn't get a break.

"No problem, fearless leader. I have the days after the New Year off. And we are going to throw one hell of a party. Excuse the language," Ryan added. He was still riding the high of the hockey charity event from the week before. He was pumped up and ready for another round.

"Perfect. Okay. We are going to throw a Christmas party this Saturday at my house. We are inviting all of the kids from Heritage House *and* any of their friends, and their friends' families – whoever they want to bring. It's an event totally dedicated to giving them – and surrounding them – with some serious Christmas magic and a whole lot of love."

Harlow waited as the girls clapped and cheered excitedly, and Ryan added a, "That is *totally* awesome."

Lisa led off for the team, "I love everything about this. What are our orders? Or, you can give me the orders and I can delegate. Either way, I'm in!"

"Great. Let's go through this together," Harlow motioned to her lists, "then Lisa, you can be in charge and you can put me to work too." Harlow slid around her desk after grabbing her notes and coffee, then sat with her team in a circle to go over all of the details.

"I have a focus area for each of you listed out in these notes." Harlow began as she handed out the sheets of paper she and Harris had worked on the day before. "Vanessa, you are all things food. The kitchens are open for use all day and cooks can come as early as they need to be ready. We'll start the event at four. You can let any available caterers know what we are doing, but if they still charge us I don't care. We aren't sparing any expense. I'm talking appetizers, turkeys, sides, munchies, and fun desserts both for kids and adults. Harris and I made tons of cookies this weekend that we can use as well so don't worry about adding any of those."

Harlow looked down at her list and didn't see the looks of intrigue shared between the group when they heard she and Harris had been baking together. When she looked up all of their attention snapped back.

"Sally and Ryan – Ryan, when you can – I want you two to handle decorations. The house already has the basics – a couple trees, lights outside, but I want you to go for it. I'm talking light it up. When these kids pull up I want their eyes to glitter with the reflection of amber glow!"

Harlow could see the gleam in Sally and Ryan's eyes as their lust for over-the-top planning would be catered to, so she went on and added to their desire, "Inside, think thick, rich garlands for the staircases and wooden trains that weave around the edges of the great room and wind around the tree. Rent as many tables as you need for the food and table decorations. Again, spare no expense. Tell people what we are doing, and if they come on board tell them we will consider using their services again in the future. Use that as a selling point."

"Jacq," Harlow turned her attention to the last of her team, "you are in charge of activities. We'll dedicate the entire second floor to games and activities. Whatever you can think of. This should include Christmas music for dancing on the inside, and a horse and sleigh ride outside. They can circle the grounds and the driveway. They are kids, so I don't think they'd last long on something farther, but they'll love every minute of the short ride. And if they want more, they can just keep circling."

Harlow paused to catch her breath before adding, "Oh, and Vanessa, let's be sure to have a hot chocolate stand outside for those waiting."

Vanessa perked up at the call-out and agreed. "You got it."

By now all five of them, Lisa included, were scribbling down notes as quickly as their hands could move to keep up with Harlow as she explained how she wanted her home to become an enchanted winter wonderland these kids would remember forever.

Who knows, she thought as she paused and waited for her team to catch up, maybe one day one of these Heritage House kids would do the same. Share the magic of Christmas for another child who needed it.

Harlow quickly sent a text to Harris letting him know the Christmas wish party plans were set in motion. She laughed when his reply read:

Operation Postmark Christmas is underway!

When she looked up she saw the knowing smirks on the faces of her team so she shooed them out without giving them a chance to give her a hard time. She yelled one final comment behind them saying, "My house is open and can be your new office for the week if you find you need to look at the space."

Harlow plopped back down and looked at Lisa, who hadn't left.

"I hope you know how incredible you are?" Lisa said when Harlow finally looked up and swiped at her latte to take another swig.

"I am not incredible. I simply have the resources and love Christmas. And I'm a sucker for kids. And in my own ridiculous bout of self-pity, I realized I needed to do something that was for more than just…me," she said, and sat up as her eyes told her something more was at stake by the look on Lisa's face. "Something is on your mind. Spill it."

Lisa grinned but something hitched when she would have started speaking and she hesitated briefly before closing her mouth again.

"Oh, now you totally have to tell me." Harlow demanded.

"I told Steve I wouldn't tell." Lisa pleaded but she knew her resolve was breaking. And she was so excited.

"Steve can beat me up later. Tell him I begged it out of you."

Lisa buried her face in her hands and spoke through them. "Okay, but try and keep it a secret."

Harlow swiped the capped end of her pen in an X across her chest when Lisa peered at her through a slit in her fingers, "Cross my heart. Secret is safe with me."

"You know how Steve and I struggled to get pregnant for so long?"

"Of course, I'm still so sorry you had to go through that. Are you having the same issues as before? Are you trying again?" Harlow had so many questions running through her mind, she had to force herself to stop and let Lisa talk.

"No, we are fine. Better than fine. But three years ago when we thought we wouldn't be able to have a baby we looked into adoption."

For the first time that morning, Harlow couldn't find words, so her head slanted to the right, questioning.

"It is *not* a quick process, and it's not cheap, but we never stopped pursuing it even when we got pregnant with Layla. And the other day, we got a call."

"You? What? You got a call, like…"

"We get to have another baby. Well, not exactly a baby, but we get to grow our family."

"Oh Lisa, I don't have words. I'm so happy for you!" Harlow lunged forward and held her dear friend who was so happy, joyful tears began to fall.

"Here," Lisa wiped her eyes when they let go of their embrace and she reached into her planner and pulled out a picture she had kept in there for safe-keeping – a constant reminder of the young boy who already held her heart.

"Do you see?" Lisa flipped the picture around so Harlow could read the name. "He's going to be at Christmas."

Harlow stared and couldn't quite believe the miracle as she read the name and said it aloud, "Mikey Andrews, age seven."

CHAPTER 22

"How did it go today?" Harlow dragged Harris through the front door after giving him a quick smack on the cheek with her painted lips. It took every ounce of her willpower not to bother Harris too much while he was at work, so now she was letting loose.

Harris closed his fingers around Harlow's and followed her in.

"The invitations are out and we've reached out to Heritage House. All of the kids have made a list of their best friends, so Helena Crawford – she runs the orphanage – is working with the school and neighbors to make sure everybody is invited and they know exactly what it's for. Mostly, she's reassuring parents that this is for the kids and it's a legitimate invite."

Harris stopped and let his eyes grow wide as he leaned in for a secret. "Apparently, around the holidays, kids can get a little eccentric and start to exaggerate the truth a little bit – and that doesn't exclude inviting friends to magical Christmas castles for a party that they can invite their friends to. An adult, unfortunately, is a little more trustworthy when it comes to inviting kids to a stranger's house. Even if it is a gorgeous mansion. Wait, sorry, I mean *magical Christmas castle.*"

"Yes," Harlow nodded seriously, "yes, I understand. And thank you, for the correction I mean. I don't want people mistaking my Christmas castle for a silly, regular old house." She smiled and flipped her feet beneath her as she plopped on the couch and pulled him down with her.

"So, what's our Christmas wish agenda today? You said you had an idea. I like your ideas."

"You don't know what my idea is yet." Harris did his best to make Harlow nervous but at this point, seeing as she was practically leaping out of her skin – like he supposed the kids would be doing in a of couple days – he decided there was no use waiting and just went for it.

"I am not trying to skimp you out of individual list items," Harris reached into his blazer pocket where he kept Harlow's Christmas letter. It was constantly with him, close to his heart throughout the days at work, and on his nightstand while he slept through the night – usually dreaming of her.

He unfolded it, and pointed to two of the lines, "one is for a winter walk in the park and the other is for buying presents. I would like to propose we embark on both in one night. Uh-ah," Harris held up a finger playfully, "hold on there. We also need to eat. Here is what I'm thinking for our evening agenda. Are you ready?"

Harlow's hands shot in the air, "Yes! Lay it on me, Christmas extraordinaire!"

Harris couldn't help his laugh. "I propose we drive downtown and park near the Christmas Market, we walk through the park and down a couple of the decked-out streets to *Louis* for dinner and dessert, then we walk back and wander the Christmas Market to see if we can find any of the presents on our list for the kids." Harris noticed Harlow was waiting to see if he was finished so he added, "Thoughts?"

Harlow sat with her hands in her lap and grinned. "Just when you think you already know how great a guy is, he goes and plans a night like that."

"I think you just said you think I'm great?" Harris joked, not wanting to be serious in the off-chance Harlow wasn't feeling the way he was about their relationship.

"Well," Harlow waved it off, "I mean, great if you think we can even get into *Louis*…"

"Reservations are at seven."

"And he's thought of everything." Harlow let the swoon fall over her but only for a second before she jumped. "Seven?" she chirped, "I need to get ready!"

Harlow was off in a dash and flying up the stairs. Harris wondered how many times in their lives together he'd try and get that same reaction out of her. The passion, compassion, and frantic excitement.

He hoped more times than he could remember by the time they were old and gray together.

—

"Tell me about your work." Harlow said as she sipped the red wine they'd ordered with dinner. They'd shared a bowl of the Cioppino and salty, crusty bread, then split a simple chocolate tart for dessert. It was the perfect way to start their night of winter walking and shopping together.

Harris mirrored her sip then sat back and shook his head. He'd never taken the time to sit back and really think about his job. As he thought about it now he realized they'd accomplished so much in just a few short years, but he hadn't paused to enjoy it.

"I love it," he said, sounding more surprised than he intended.

Harlow smiled and asked jokingly, "You didn't know that you loved it?"

"Ha, it seems silly doesn't it?" Harris admitted. "For the longest time, even as a kid, I remember thinking *I'm going to make something of myself and this company.* We've done that – multiple times over. But tonight, looking back on it, it's always been great. We are profitable. We are sustainable."

Harris looked down searching, wondering how it was he hadn't realized it before.

Harlow placed her hand on his and said, "I have a feeling you've lent a great deal to that."

She couldn't quite believe what she was hearing. Harlow had imagined Harris as the ultimate professional. Never ceasing his progress or movement forward. Never pausing for a woman or a family. Always worried about the bottom line. Yet, here he was, realizing maybe he didn't have to try so hard.

But just as she started to feel hopeful, Harris continued.

"Once we finish this collaboration with Pro Feed – you remember Calvin from the charity event?"

Harlow's spirit plummeted in an instant and all she could offer was a single nod in acknowledgment. She slid her hand away from Harris' and replaced it on the stem of her wine glass, wishing it was full to the brim.

"We just have to make one final push. One more sprint, and we'll be there. It'll be a lot of work. Long hours, days, weeks, months. But then," Harris looked up, his eyes radiant with a competitive gleam, "we will have created the perfect company. We'll *never* have another worry in the world."

She knew her smile was forced, but she also knew she had no right to be disappointed. The letter, the postbox – all of it – was run by Harris' company. He was simply the man who had been assigned to fulfill her Christmas wishes. He would do this task as he would any other – tirelessly to achieve the best results. Then he would move on to the next important venture.

So, she thought, she would accept that, enjoy this time and the wonderful Christmas party for an amazing, hopeful group of children, then move on with her own life.

"I'm happy for you and proud of what you've been able to accomplish." Harlow said, offering her true feelings – because she was proud of him.

She just also happened to be in love with him. Sometimes, she supposed, the truth and love didn't quite align. He would accept her pride in him, but he was unable to accept her love in the way she wanted him to.

"Thanks," Harris said, noting the shift in her tone, the seriousness, so he added, "It really means a lot to me – that you're proud."

Harlow finished her glass of red and breathed deeply.

"Okay," she said, "should we head to the park then embark on some holiday shopping?"

"Let's do it," Harris said, as he did the same and finished off the remaining droplets of his own glass.

As Harlow and Harris walked slowly down the sidewalk, taking in lamps adorned with evergreen wreaths and trees with lights wound around them, she thought it felt colder than it had on their way over. Or, perhaps a little of the optimistic warmth the feeling of love had wrapped around her earlier, had taken on a lonely chill.

They'd walked along the road until they reached the picturesque Rice Park. It looked like a glowing Currier and Ives painting.

The path leading them through the middle of the park was lined with curved black iron benches and matching old-fashioned lamp posts that had been kissed by drifts of snow. The beautifully trimmed trees that had lost their leaves for the season now had a new adornment with what seemed like millions of little twinkling star lights.

The world could have gone completely dark, she thought, but these dazzling trees could have lit it all on their own.

They passed lovers walking arm-in-arm or holding hands, groups of friends laughing on their way to dinner or a play, and people who just wanted to enjoy the beautiful evening alone or to walk their happy dogs.

How could somebody walk through a moment like this and not fall in love with the season and everything it represented? Harlow thought, grinning at a child and a puppy rolling in the snow to their right. It made something like work seem so insignificant, and she wondered, how it was possible that somebody as kind and generous as Harris didn't see the same thing.

Just beyond the park they saw the glow of the Christmas Market and heard the sound of music and cheerful voices stretching over to them, reaching out and pulling them in. When they heard the upbeat beginning of *Step Into Christmas* and the crowd cheer at the sound, Harlow and Harris looked excitedly at each other and hurried their pace.

People were ordering beers and ciders, gazing at homemade trinkets and gifts, and many of them were there to do nothing but enjoy the magnetic energy.

"This is amazing." Harlow said, spinning to take in all of the little shops and food stands.

There were glass ornaments, ceramics, and clay pottery. Hand-carved bowls and trays, and cute little wooden toys she couldn't keep herself from wandering toward.

By the time they had circled the market once they had bags filled with knitted hats and gloves, adorable jackets, cozy indoor slippers, and a toy or two for each child who would be at the Christmas party. They'd even purchased an ornament for every person that would be in attendance – including the staff.

Harlow decided it would be a new tradition. Every magical Christmas party going forward would have its own ornament, and it would be given away as a gift. Something special for everyone to remember the time together.

When they thought they were finished, Harlow and Harris began to make their way out, but slowed as they started past a European pancake stand.

They had, only two hours ago, eaten a delectable meal. But something about the potato pancakes and German pretzels called to them. And without speaking they turned and stepped into the line, unable to resist.

CHAPTER 23

The next day, The Hill was energized and swarming with movement and chaos as teams moved in and out, preparing for the weekend event.

Christmas Eve was exactly one week away, Harlow grinned at the thought as she looked around, so she didn't feel even the slightest bit of guilt when she told her staff to hold off on the removal of the decorations until after the New Year. After all, there wasn't any sense in removing it before then. She might as well enjoy the spectacular display straight through the holiday.

Lisa walked up behind Harlow, who stood on the second floor overlooking the frenzy below.

"How are you feeling today?" Lisa asked, wondering if a new day had given her friend a little more optimism than she'd had the day before. Lisa had been tired, but when the call came in late last night she knew she had to answer. So she'd sat and listened to Harlow rationalize why she couldn't tell Harris how she felt about him.

Harlow didn't make eye contact and continued staring below with a face of resolve.

"I'm feeling..." Harlow stood a bit straighter, "I'm feeling determined."

She turned to face Lisa and her face softened. "I have to be determined. If not, I'll remember that I'm in love with Harris. I know what you're going to say. But if I tell him, I'll be forcing him to choose. If he chooses to embark on a romance with me, he'll resent me for pulling him away from work." Harlow lifted her hands at the possibilities, then let them fall with the inevitable consequences. "Or worse, I resent *him* for working too much. Either way we'll be better off without the heartbreak we could have avoided."

Harlow turned and looked out again resting her hands on the wooden railing. "I know what it's like to love people who want to be somewhere else."

Lisa's heart broke a little bit for her friend. If only her family knew how much she missed them.

Lisa turned and stood next to Harlow, looking out over the same mess of preparation. Harlow wanted people present in this house so badly. To fill the emptiness, she had literally invited more than one hundred strangers into it. Strangers who, by the end of the Christmas party, would feel like a part of the family, Lisa thought. Her mission would be accomplished.

Harlow felt the bump of Lisa's shoulder. "Come on," Lisa said. "Let's test the hot chocolate and wander the most magnificent Christmas wonderland I've ever seen."

As they walked the grounds with the rich scent of chocolate billowing from their cups, they took it in.

A small tractor was pressing a path of snow around the house and through the awning of the carriage house – a house that looked like a cute miniature version of the mansion sitting off to the left. And, they noted, the carriage house was being prepped with white twinkling lights of its own.

More evergreen trees were being carried in by workers who volunteered to make the delivery from the nursery. They'd donated all of the remaining trees that hadn't sold for the season to the party. It was so close to Christmas they'd kept only a few behind on their lot for last-minute shoppers or Christmas emergencies.

Harlow and Lisa followed the trees in, walking on the brown paper they'd laid on the floor in an attempt to keep it clean from the tracks of snow and needles that were left behind.

The great room was filled with wooden nutcrackers, airplanes, and train sets that would be linked together to form a track that would allow the train to chug around the room in an endless loop.

Glittery red, gold, and silver presents were being wrapped and bowed, and little tags were being adorned with kids and family names, then signed from Santa.

As they wandered to the kitchen they saw silver and wooden dessert trays and tiers meticulously placed along the length of the island. Punch bowls and drink trays were prepped in the butler's kitchen through the two-way swinging door, and small, delicate wreaths hung from each cabinet door.

Harlow tried to focus on the planning and decorating, but as they walked through the kitchen she felt the warmth of the kiss Harris had placed on her cheek just feet away when they had made dinner together. A kiss that felt so tender, so filled with emotion.

She'd wanted to wrap her arms around him and simply hold him. The kind of embrace that made you feel safe. The kind that made you want to hold tighter, because if you did, you might push the love you had for that person right into them. Then you hoped with everything inside of you they could feel it.

When Harlow stopped her movement forward, she looked at Lisa. "I have to tell him."

"I know you do, sweetie."

"Not telling him will be worse than never knowing. What will come of it? – I have no idea," Harlow shrugged and shook her head, "but I have to try."

Harlow looked around at everything that still had to be done.

"I have everything here under control. You go," Lisa said, offering a comforting hand on Harlow's arm.

"Thank you." Sincerity poured out with the words. "Lisa, I'm so grateful for you."

Lisa smiled and said her thank you in the only way she knew how: "Me too. Love you, Harlow. You're the best friend I've ever had."

The two friends hugged, then Harlow spun around, taking one last look at the holiday transformation, and skipped out of the room.

Harris would be at work, but something was telling her love couldn't wait.

CHAPTER 24

Harris was on a mission. He had work to do and it wasn't going to be easy. The timeline was tight – almost impossible – but he was going to get it done, whatever the cost.

When he saw Brandon in his office, head down, he knew he was going to be the cause of serious disruption. But he'd get Brandon on board. And, he thought, he'd better get his dad in the room, too. His dad had made a lot of promises on Harris' behalf, so he'd have to do some explaining to people who had a lot of influence, and who would be much more impacted.

Harris knocked on Brandon's door and received a blank stare at the interruption. Harris nearly laughed at Brandon's face, that was clearly still lost in whatever he was working on.

"Brandon," he started, "do you have time for a quick meeting?" Harris asked and continued as he saw Brandon was about to tell him he was really busy – and Harris knew he was. "It won't take long, and it's important."

Brandon's blank look of confusion turned to intrigue with the lift of a single brow and he pushed away from his desk. Usually when Harris used 'It's important,' it was.

Harris led Brandon away from their own offices toward his dad's. It was Harris' turn to be confused as they found the door closed rather than open in welcome. He knocked twice on the clouded glass pane that had *Charles Porter* etched in the middle.

The two men stared at each other from the outside and couldn't hide their boyish grins as they heard the unmistakable sound of Santa's laughter mixed with the booming sound of Charles' baritone howl. They shook their heads at the grown men sharing a youthful bout of cheerfulness, and pushed in when they heard two voices invite them in.

Santa and Charles were perched on chairs facing each other with faces so red they looked like cinnamon Lollipops. Their grins were wide and their eyes bright. They looked like a couple of kids who'd been caught causing mischief and having a little too much fun. Harris didn't know if he should feel bad for breaking it up or that he wasn't invited to join in.

"Dad, Santa. How are both of you today?" Harris asked as he and Brandon walked in and took their places next to the two men.

"Well," Santa perked, "I sure can't complain. I've heard about the Christmas party you and Harlow are throwing and I couldn't be more overjoyed." Santa looked to each of the men enthusiastically bouncing his head up and down in agreement. "If you wouldn't mind, I would like to make an appearance. Maybe bring a special gift or two for the youngsters?"

"Yes," Harris said, not realizing Santa's excitement had bewitched him, taking him along as if on a joyful sleighride. "That would be great. The kids would love it. And Harlow, well, she'd be thrilled."

Charles and Santa eyed each other in a shared secret at Harris' tone when he mentioned the name of the woman who'd stolen his heart.

Harris didn't seem to notice and thought, it's now or never. He might as well let them in on the mission and the hit the company would take by forcing a delay. Maybe if Santa was here his excitement would soften the blow.

"Actually, I'm glad you're all here." He looked to Brandon, "And thanks for taking the time to stop what you were working on – I know you're busy."

The men leaned in, wondering what it could be that would make them even more pressed for time than they already were with the collaboration. Though Santa didn't seem worried, Harris noted, when he stole a look in his direction after taking in the faces of his dad and Brandon.

"I'd like to delay the collaboration."

Harris waited as faces processed and registered. His dad showed surprise – the happy kind. Brandon showed the same, but with a little more defeat lining the edges of his eyes.

"It will still happen," Harris said, assuring Brandon the work he'd done so far wouldn't be lost. But he needed Brandon because he was the best. His planning, organization, and brilliancy with logistics were exactly the skillsets needed for something that was more important.

"Well, son, what are you thinking?"

The men looked from Charles back to Harris.

"I'd like to use some resources to fulfill one of our Christmas wishes from a postbox letter," Harris said, happy it didn't sound as ridiculous as he thought it might when he said it out loud. Though, he thought, they might disagree seeing as the request came from him. It wasn't like him to slow business progress for…anything.

Charles nodded for Harris to go on when nobody made a sound.

Harris pulled Harlow's Christmas letter out of his pocket and unfolded it to reveal the pictures inside. He eyed the worn edges and the ragged look of them from his need to pull it out throughout his day just to see her face. Harris filed through the familiar pictures once more until he found the picture of the entire family wearing ugly Christmas sweaters with their names printed on the front. Then handed it to Brandon.

Brandon accepted the picture and looked down, unable to suppress the grin caused by the terrible sweaters they were wearing. Then looked to Harris once more.

"I need you to track down the people in this picture. Those are their names. Last name is Hill. They shouldn't be hard to look up, but they might be hard to find. And," he added with a shrug knowing the next part might be impossible, "I want you to try and get them flights home by Christmas. Do and say whatever you can to get them to agree. I'm assuming they will bring their families, so make sure every member has a ticket."

Harris looked to his dad for approval then to Brandon who was looking to Charles as well, searching for the same go-ahead.

"You heard him," Charles said to Brandon, "spare no expense. Let's get the family home for Christmas."

—

Nancy had given Harlow the directions up to the office. She'd still had to sign in, but Nancy said an escort wasn't needed for somebody as special as Harlow. And that Harris would be sure to see her, no matter what he was working on.

Harlow smiled at the recall of the quick conversation, and took a right out of the elevator as instructed. If she walked straight forward she would run right into Harris' office.

Harlow looked around and saw Christmas decorations scattered around the floor, and noted many of the cubicles had their own spaces decorated for the season. A personal touch, she thought, when you had to be away from home throughout the day. She did the same with her office, surrounding herself with pictures and decorations of her own.

Harris' voice had echoed out of a room to her left, so she altered her course and slowly navigated toward the sound, smiling at the enthusiastic tone. She wasn't spying as she inched closer, or at least that wasn't her intention, she simply wanted to take in the Harris she only had the chance to imagine he'd be in a work environment. Cool and calm energy, but the ultimate go-getter. People would respect and follow him, she knew. She would have done the same had he been her superior.

But when she leaned in her heart sank at what she heard.

"There is *this*. *Nothing* else matters." Harris' voice was laced with finality. "Whatever you have to do, even if it means we work straight through Christmas Eve."

Harlow felt the tears pool in her eyes as she turned to lean her back against the wall. The reality was exactly as she thought it would be. He would do anything for the job. And, she thought, as his words slammed into her mind, 'straight through Christmas Eve,' she shouldn't expect him at their Christmas party.

This feeling, of her chest caving in, was what she was trying to avoid. The pain and heartbreak of knowing Harris was a businessman, not a family man. He loved his family, sure, but loving the one he had and dreaming of one of his own were two heartbreakingly different things.

Harlow lifted herself off the wall, adjusted her jacket and bag, and turned to walk out.

She couldn't worry about heartbreak right now. So she would keep the love she had for Harris to herself, cherish the rest of the time they would have, then move on with hopes of a happy new year and a mind that would forget how much she longed to be with him. Then Harlow started her walk back down.

She had a Christmas party to plan.

CHAPTER 25

Eight messages had come in from Harris the next day. One wondering how she was doing, and how the party was coming together. Another letting her know all of the invitations and transportation logistics to and from the party were taken care of. A sweet message to tell her he was thinking about her, and hoping to confirm their hot chocolate and movie night. And a final one asking if everything was okay since he hadn't heard from her.

Harlow sat in the library. The decorating had finished in the majestic room an hour earlier, so it was one place she could be alone because it wasn't swarming with people. She'd closed the doors, set her phone on the table next to the high-backed leather armchair, sat, and stared at it.

Everything in her heart and body was urging her to pick it up and write back to him. That yes, everything was on schedule. The house was even more beautiful than she could've imagined it in her most magical and wonderful dreams. That yes, she wanted to see him tonight more than anything, but no, she wasn't okay, because she was in love with him and he didn't love her back.

So, her mind told her no, and she let the phone sit.

As she looked around the library she couldn't believe the holiday elegance. Rich, velvety, deep green ribbons draped from the floor-to-ceiling bookcases that lined the walls. Huge bows twisted and curled with every new shelf, and each long pane in the wall of windows dangled a wreath with the same velvety bow topping them all.

White and silver snow globes of different shapes and sizes were scattered, but beautifully placed, throughout the room. She noticed many of them were her own, or ones her parents or siblings had left behind when they moved.

Harlow picked one off of the table next to her and looked at the children inside with shimmering snow fluttering around them. The tiny glass figures had built a snowman with a crooked carrot nose. All of them laughing, and when Harlow turned the silver crank on the bottom, it looked as if they might have been singing along to the happy chimes of *Frosty the Snowman.*

As she watched the children play and listened to the music, even surrounded by all of the people moving in and out of her home, she had never felt more alone. She missed her family. And, she admitted, it had only been two days, but she missed Harris.

Harlow wondered, just for a minute, if it was worth finishing her Christmas wishes. She could pick up the phone and tell Harris she had too much to do, and their planned night together for a movie had to be cancelled. Or, she thought, she could just enjoy being lucky enough to have had somebody willing to fulfill her Christmas wishes at all.

That idea hung in the cinnamon-scented air as she contemplated.

Maybe, she decided as she pulled her feet onto the chair with her, she should be grateful. And she picked up the phone, opened Harris' messages, and tapped out her reply.

CHAPTER 26

Harlow held her body while laughing at the seriousness on Harris' face as he tried to decide. She had whittled the movie choices down to four. He to three. She to two.

And now, he was faced with the ultimate decision of picking the final movie.

Harris looked up, bewildered at how hard it was to choose. Deciding between white, dark, or milk chocolate to fill their hot mugs was easy. A question to add peppermint, almond, or butterscotch flavoring was simple. Toasted marshmallows, chocolate shavings, or chopped pecans for a garnish – a no-brainer. But this?

He was having to decide between Dr. Seuss and Bing Crosby. Cartoon or real life. Both classics. But both on inarguable opposite ends of the Christmas spectrum.

Harris realized, deciding to approve five thousand dollars in airline tickets earlier that day had been easier.

"I just – I can't do it." Harris held up the DVDs, one in each hand, looking helpless with pouting puppy-dog-eyes.

"I need help," he finally admitted, getting another round of giggles out of Harlow, who'd finally composed herself enough to speak.

"I have an idea," Harlow said, taking two deep breaths to steady her voice, and making sure she wouldn't burst into round two at the look on his face.

"What if we started with *The Grinch?* It's a light classic, it's quick, and it's fun. Then we can get a refill and put in *White Christmas* and settle in for the long haul?"

Harris' hands dropped to his sides, the DVDs falling with them. "Why didn't I think of that?" he asked. "It's brilliant."

Harlow lifted her head at the compliment and said, "It doesn't happen often, but when my brilliance sets in, it is really something."

This got Harris to laugh along with her, and he turned to slide the movie in, then settled next to Harlow beneath a white Sherpa blanket with his dark hot chocolate with whipped cream and chopped pecans.

—

They sang the wonky words they knew – and hummed the ones they didn't – while watching all of the Whos in Whoville as they held hands and swayed around the tree. Then they waited until all of the credits had scrolled through before saying a word or making a move.

"It is just *so good*, right?" Harlow asked, amazed at how a funny-looking green thing could make her so emotional.

"So good," Harris agreed. "So, *so* good."

Harlow heard her phone come alive as the vibrations buzzed her phone across the coffee table. She didn't recognize the number, but picked the phone up and offered, "How about I'll take this and you can get us refills?"

"Sounds like another good plan. Same order?"

"Same order," she confirmed while swiping her phone to answer. She grinned as she heard Harris confirm their orders as he walked away from her.

"One white hot chocolate with peppermint and marshmallows – coming up!"

"Hello?" Harlow answered into the phone.

"Hi, may I please speak to Harlow Hill?" the voice asked other the other end.

"This is Harlow, how can I help you?"

"This might sound like a strange request, but I'm wondering where you'll be for Christmas this year? I'm asking on behalf of Harris Porter."

Harlow looked toward the kitchen where she heard the faint whistle of *The Grinch* song Harris must have gotten stuck in his head.

"Ah," she shifted from one foot to the other, unsure of where this was going, or if she should answer the stranger at all, "I'll be here, in Minnesota."

"Oh, *thank all the elves in the North Pole.*" The voice on the other end managed to sound exhausted and relieved at the same time.

"Can I ask who this is and why you're asking?"

"Of course. I'm Brandon Carlson. I work for Mr. Porter. He has to finalize work on a Christmas letter so he can get a big project started at work. I'm helping him out so once it's all over we can get approval and hit the ground running. We can't move forward until it's done."

"I see," Harlow said, dropping to the couch.

"So, you'll be here, then? In St. Paul, right? At The Hill for Christmas?"

The voice – Brandon – sounded more optimistic than he had earlier. Perhaps excited that he'd be able to move on, just like Harris would after Saturday. The Christmas party would mark the last of her wishes – of the ones that she'd kept on the list.

"I will be here," she confirmed and clicked the phone screen to end the call.

"Okay!" Harris cheered as he walked back in. "Two delectable hot chocolates for the merry drinking! One for you," Harris bent to carefully hand her a mug overflowing with giant marshmallows and tiny peppermint pieces, "and, one for me."

Harris sat and looked over to her when she didn't respond, concern immediately flooding in. "Harlow, what is it? Are you okay?"

She forced a smile and looked toward him, telling herself everything was as it should be, that nothing in her life was changing or out of place. The holidays would end and she'd go back to things as they were – normal. Normal, she thought, and alone.

"You know what?" Harlow started and set her hot chocolate on the table. "I'm really sorry, but I'm not feeling well. I think I should probably head to bed." It wasn't a lie. She wanted nothing more than to cocoon herself in the comfort of heavy blankets and fall asleep. Then maybe the looming sadness and nausea wouldn't take her over.

"What can I do?" Harris knelt before her, looking over her as if he could examine the pain and make her better.

"Nothing at all. I'm sure it's just exhaustion from everything that's been going on. I'd rather rest now so I can be ready and well for Saturday's party." She looked Harris in the eye. "I think it might be best if you leave for the night."

Harlow didn't allow for Harris to argue.

"Thank you," she continued, "for executing all of the wishes on my Christmas list. It really has meant the world to me to get to live all of those moments again."

Harlow stood and walked away, leaving him no choice but to follow her to the door. He couldn't stay, as it wasn't his house – even though when he was here with her it felt like home. And, she wasn't feeling well; he couldn't magically make her feel better. But if given the chance he'd move Christmas Day to do it. Even the nagging in the back of his mind telling him something was wrong wasn't giving him a good excuse to stay.

He slid his jacket on, then his hat and mittens, and turned to where she was standing next to the open door.

"Good night, Harris."

Harris couldn't help but feel like she was telling him "Goodbye" rather than "Good night." But he leaned in and placed a kiss on her cheek, then walked into the night.

He stopped just outside, instantly frozen as the cold rushed into him, and said, "I hope you feel better. Sleep well,

Harlow." He tried for a grin and added, "I hope you dream of sugarplums as they dance in your head."

Then   he   turned   and   didn't   look   back.

CHAPTER 27

They were ready. Harlow couldn't believe it.

The team had managed to pull together the most magnificent, Christmassy, party-plan of all time. She was overwhelmed and overjoyed at the dedication of her team and the generosity of all of the vendors and shops they'd worked with. Nearly all of them had donated the rentals, supplies, and goods. And when they were asked to pay, the discounts were so large she knew the companies weren't making a profit, simply covering the cost of expenses.

How wonderful people could be, she mused.

Harlow looked at her phone to check the time and saw they had about an hour before the kids and families would start to arrive. She also noted that Harris hadn't called her back.

The way she'd forced him out was causing her more guilt than she expected. She wanted to talk to him, to simply ask what the call was about. She would let him know that even though it made her feel badly, she understood the pressures of work. She'd felt it early on in her own career, when she was trying to prove herself to her own family.

Harlow had tried his cell phone, his office phone, and talked to Nancy twice a day, every day. The only answer she'd gotten was that Harris was working diligently on an urgent matter that was taking all of his time. And that she was sure he'd give her a call as soon as he had a minute to spare.

"Still nothing?" Lisa asked as she joined Harlow at the dining room table.

"Still nothing," Harlow said, confirming her friend's question for the second time that day. If she hadn't been depressed about the situation, the ritual could have been funny. Their comical new way of greeting one another.

Still nothing? Still nothing.

Lisa reached a hand across the table runner, weaving through the legs of brass-colored, metal deer that stood regally the length of the table in a herd, and rested it on Harlow's.

"No matter what happens – what you've done here, with this house, and for these kids – you should be so proud of yourself. *I* am so proud of you," Lisa said, her smile genuine and full of love. "You are giving these kids something so wonderful. You're giving my child," Lisa's voice quivered with emotion, "the best Christmas."

Harlow turned her hand over and held Lisa's. "No, *you* are giving him the best Christmas. This is simply a means of delivering the message. Are you ready?"

Harlow didn't have to explain the question. Lisa knew she was asking if she was ready to take in another beloved child.

"I am tired, exhausted, and living on two hours of sleep and fumes. But I've never been more ready for anything in my life."

"Yeah, you are," Harlow agreed, then asked again, this time referring to the party. "Okay then, are you ready?"

"As   I'll   ever   be."

CHAPTER 28

The frenzied sound of children's laughter and happiness rang through the sturdy walls and carried to where Harlow, Lisa, the firm's staff, and all of the hired chefs and hosts were waiting. When Harlow turned to see if they could hear the excitement that would be bursting through the doors in a matter of seconds, she saw every face mirroring hers in a smile so big, so filled with hopefulness and cheer, she could hardly keep her own excitement contained.

The doorbell chime sounded like it never had before – like a bell so beautiful it could be heard in the heavens and letting the whole world hear the love in its ringing.

Harlow turned the knob and swung open the door, and as she did she was greeted with a chorus of children yelling, "Merry Christmas!" then all of the kids danced and shouted while spinning in circles to take in the lights and the spectacle that was waiting just on the other side of the door.

"Merry Christmas!" everybody on the inside sang back. Then Harlow laughed, looked at the rosy, eager faces, and exclaimed, "Are you ready?"

Harlow stepped aside and waved them in as they shouted "Yes!" while passing.

Some squealed as they found a favorite ornament, a few grabbed their friends' hands and ran to explore, and others stood in bewildered fascination at the wintery world of Christmas they had just walked into.

One boy walked up to the tree with his mouth gaping, then twirled to take in all of the magnificence. Harlow swore that as he turned she saw the reflection of the wonder in his wide eyes, and in that moment, she had a feeling that warmed her heart completely.

"Hi," Harlow offered, quietly moving toward him so they could stand and stare together.

"Hi." The boy's response was drawn out in awe.

"What do you think?" Harlow asked, looking around with the boy as she followed his eyes.

He turned once more and finally paused when he met her face-to-face, after she knelt down to match his height. His innocent smile started small but grew as his eyes brightened.

"It's a miracle," he whispered.

Harlow marveled at his description and his perfect innocence, then nodded in agreement.

"I have a feeling this is only the beginning."

The boy beamed and giggled in the way only a young child could. Before she knew what was happening, he lunged at her, gave her a hug, and with the gentle sound of innocence and youth said, "This is already the best Christmas of my life."

Then he raced off laughing and shouting with the other children.

Harlow looked over to see Lisa watching with her hands over her mouth, not believing what she just witnessed, so overjoyed in the moment she couldn't get herself to move in and join them.

When Harlow crossed to her she offered her own embrace.

"How is he?" Lisa asked through unsteady breaths as Harlow held her, knowing in a few short days that precious boy would be hers.

"He's absolutely perfect in every way."

———

Kids shouted, laughed, and raced excitedly from room to room, chasing after friends and running with new toys held high. Parents and friends sat in the great room, around the dining table, and in small pockets of the house that were designed for casual conversation.

Harlow couldn't stay in the same place too long, because she felt like she would miss small special moments that were happening in every room. As she walked and greeted the guests, she was thanked more than once for her generosity, and many times was offered help or payment. It gave her the greatest pleasure to tell them having the house full – as it should be – was payment enough.

"Harlow Hill?" A woman's voice caught her as she passed the library.

When she stopped she watched a woman as she handed a Christmas book to a young girl and slid another child off her lap, letting them know she'd be back in just a moment.

"Yes?" Harlow said, "Welcome, how can I help you? Can I get you anything?"

The woman reached out for Harlow's hands as she shook her head. "No," she said. "I – we – don't need a single thing. This night has been blessing enough. I'm Helena Crawford, I run Heritage House." Helena introduced herself, as she had only heard wonderful things about Harlow through her communications with Harris.

"Helena!" Harlow said, brightening as recognition came to her. "Oh, I'm so happy we could do this for the kids."

"We do well there – at the house I mean – but this…" Helena looked back toward the girls who giggled when they were caught spying, "this is more than we could have ever imagined. Thank you."

Harlow smiled, and with every ounce of her being meant her next words, "I should be the one thanking you. This night is the best of my entire life."

When hours passed and Harlow didn't think she had an ounce of emotional energy left, she walked to the door when the bell chimed.

She was ready to surprise the same little rascals that had hidden around a column from her the last time she answered the door, but this time when she opened it, her heart found a little extra room in it to feel.

"Charles and Barbara! What are you doing here?" Harlow exclaimed as she walked into their outstretched arms.

"Harris told us about what you were doing for these kids and we couldn't miss it! *Wouldn't* miss it. Not for a single thing."

"I'm so…I don't have any more happy words that I haven't already used tonight." Harlow shrugged. "Maybe, let's go with…*overjoyed!*"

Charles and Barbara laughed and followed her in, and it was their turn to gape.

"In my wildest imagination I couldn't have dreamed the beauty of this," Barbara said as she let her coat drop from her shoulders into her husband's hands. "It's like a Christmas fairytale."

Barbara walked to Harlow and placed a hand on her cheek. "My dear, this, and you, are exquisite in every way. Inside and out."

Harlow didn't say anything, simply let her head rest on Barbara's hand and relish the motherly tenderness.

"We didn't bring anything exciting for the kids – from what Harris said they all had gifts to open. So," Charles looked a little bashful but continued, "we thought these could maybe help them in the future. More of a long-term gift."

Charles held out white envelopes tied with a simple gold ribbon. Harlow received them and looked down, wondering what they could have brought. Her questioning eyes looked back to Charles.

"Harris gave us a list of all the kids that would be in attendance – and the ones who wouldn't. We have a scholarship fund at our company. It's used to help kids pursue a college, or trade-school, or whatever kind of schooling they might want to attend after high school.

"That, there," Charles pointed to the envelopes in Harlow's hand, "is full funding for each kid. So long as they maintain passing grades, we'll keep paying for classes."

"Oh my God. I just–I don't know what to say." Harlow's words tripped over each other as they stumbled out.

"Then all you have to say is 'Thank you.' And know it was your generosity with this," Barbara motioned to the rooms filled with laughter behind her, "that encouraged us to want to help. I hope you'll understand and respect that we'd like the donation to remain anonymous."

"Anything. Anything at all that you wish is what we'll do. Thank you. Thank you so much for this!"

—

Harlow sat in the top of the carriage house where she used to hide as a young girl. It was the one place she could go when she and her brother and sister would play hide and seek. Back then, she'd chosen that hiding spot because she knew her sister and brother were too scared to go up there, so she'd win the game. Now, she knew nobody else would find her because they didn't know it existed.

She watched her house and the grounds from a distance. It was a perfect scene that played out in slow motion.

The Clydesdale horse and carriage were circling as riders in the back sipped hot chocolate and pointed at decorations and bright lights. People flashed in and out of windowed frames as they moved throughout the house. She watched them laugh and hug, kids chase and dance, and lean heads back as they enjoyed a savory meal or Christmassy treat.

They had done it, she thought. They had fulfilled every wish on her Christmas list.

Well, all but one. But she'd taken *love* off docket. It wasn't something you asked for, or something that somebody could provide you. It had to be given freely. An offering of the heart.

Harris, who was nowhere to be found, had stolen hers without even trying. Yet, she thought as she rested her chin on her knees, he'd never asked for it and had never told her to give it to him. So maybe...

"It's kind of a cold night to be up there, don't you think?"

Harlow leaned forward and looked down where the carriage house overhang bridged the snow-covered stone path below.

"Santa? How did you find me?" Harlow asked, not even trying to hide her surprise.

"I would give you the 'I see you when you're sleeping, and know when you're awake' line, but for some reason when I do that people always look a little more worried than impressed."

She couldn't help but laugh at the rosy old man, who couldn't for the life of him figure out why he would get that reaction – and worked her way down to meet him.

Santa led off ignoring Harlow's question. "I thought I'd come out tonight and join the fun. I went inside, it really is something. And I've seen a lot of Christmases." Santa nodded his head as if he were navigating the memories of Christmases past for comparison. "I think just about everybody is going to get something wonderful for Christmas this year. Not all of the gifts are things, but they are all exactly what's needed."

Harlow grinned but kept her face forward, looking in the same direction as Santa – not at anything in particular, just out and over, taking everything in.

"I couldn't help but notice you didn't get everything that *you* wanted this year for Christmas," Santa said, looking toward her.

"But I did," Harlow said, "I was given everything on my list," then she motioned to the house, "and so much more."

"See, that right there. That willingness to give, that's why it's always been so easy."

Harlow turned to Santa, her eyes searching.

"So easy to give to you, is what I mean. No, now don't say anything, I'm Santa Claus. I see you when you're sleeping and I know when you're awake."

Santa tested the phrase on Harlow to see if her reaction would be different than the others. He peered at her and accepted her reaction. A questioning look was better than terrified. It was always so hard for adults to believe.

"Anyway," he went on, "you are correct, everything on your list was answered. But it seems to me there was one thing missing from your list this year?"

"How could you-? Or, how do you-?" Harlow couldn't quite find the words to ask a question that should have been impossible. How could he have known she'd asked to fall in love?

"Well, I'm just here to let you know, there's still time. Christmas letters filled with wishes are valid right up to Christmas Eve."

Santa clapped his gloved hands together snapping Harlow out of her stare.

"Well, I should get going. There is a lot to do over the next couple of days. I can't waste a single second. They are precious."

Harlow watched Santa walk away from her. He stopped briefly to pet and talk to the Clydesdale and she swore she saw the horse laugh. Then he vanished around the sleigh and out of sight.

She stood for only a second longer before sprinting inside. She ran past Lisa, who was sitting on the floor putting a Christmas puzzle together with Mikey, and threw her hands in the air in a silent cheer when Lisa looked up and smiled.

She ran down the hall and found the library, then raced to the desk where she'd left her letter paper and envelopes. She rushed around the long wooden frame and dropped herself into the chair.

Harlow stared at the blank sheet, knowing what she was about to do – again – was *still* insane.

Slowing her movements, Harlow delicately pulled the top drawer open, reached for a pen, then gently pushed it closed. She uncapped the pen, placed it on the paper and wrote:

Dear Santa,

Merry Christmas, and a happy and peaceful holiday season to you.

Harlow smiled as she recalled, and wrote exactly what she had in the first Christmas wish.

I still am a person who is not in need of anything in this life. I am still blessed beyond measure. So again, if you must choose between this letter and those of others, choose theirs. Their Christmas wish is much more important than mine.

However, if you find you have some extra time, and feel like adding a little more Christmas magic to my life, I would love for you to read this.

I would like nothing else but this.

10. To fall in love

From a hopeful believer in the Magic of Christmas,

Harlow Hill

CHAPTER 29

It was Christmas Eve, and Harris was at work. And if he didn't leave in the next ten minutes, his mom was going to kill him.

It definitely wasn't the first time he'd worked on Christmas Eve, or had been late to the festivities. Or hadn't gone at all for that matter. Then what made this Christmas so different?

Harris let the question linger as he put together a final email correspondence to Calvin Crane. Letting him, and his Pro Feed team, know they'd have a slight delay – no, not a delay, he thought – a purposeful push of the launch so co-workers, friends, and families of those who would be included in the collaboration could enjoy the holiday season and the start of a New Year with the ones they loved.

Even as he hit send, after signing off with a hope that everybody had a Merry Christmas, he couldn't quite believe *he* was the one who wanted this. It brought his mind back to the question at hand, and he knew the answer.

Harlow was responsible for his change of heart. The weather outside could be, and has been, bitter cold and frightful, but she managed to warm him to the core.

In a few short weeks she had taught him there wasn't any amount of material things or money that could replace the feeling of love and family. The feelings he had for her – and the future of the family he wanted.

Harris shook his head at the woman who, without a doubt, loved her beautiful mansion. She cherished the memories it offered and the history it represented. But Harris knew, if forced to choose between a chance to share her life with somebody and The Hill, she'd give it – and everything else – up in a heartbeat.

"I figured I'd find you here."

Harris looked up to see his dad standing in the doorway of his office. Charles' jacket was still zipped to his chin and his silly floppy hat that made him look a little like Elmer Fudd was still snug around his head.

"Before I wouldn't have taken offense to that," Harris said as he lifted a guilty eyebrow. "But this year…the guilt in realizing how many holidays I've missed because of work is falling on me like heavy and unrelenting snowfall. An avalanche to be exact."

Charles shrugged, not wanting his son to feel too badly about it, just thankful Harris realized it at all. He pulled his hat off and put his disheveled hair back in place, then unzipped his jacket and set it on the chair next to the one he took.

"I was the same way once," Charles said. The admission had Harris looking confused and wondering what his dad was talking about.

"When my dad," Charles rolled a finger forward to better acknowledge the relationship, "your Grandpa, Arnold, found success in this company, I was old enough to notice."

Charles nodded before continuing. "Like you, I noticed the shift in our lifestyle. Only, we *really* hadn't had money before that. And I liked the luxuries our new life afforded."

"The generations before us might not have suffered," Charles went on, "but they went without, in hopes and dreams this place would one day make something of itself. We are the lucky ones who get to eat the fruits of their labor. I almost realized it too late. Almost lost your mother because of it."

Harris looked down, not ashamed, but knowing he should have known the difference in his own life between not having and having. And that he might very well be in the same position of losing Harlow – maybe he already had – because of it.

"I'm afraid it's my fault. We – your mother and I – never sat you down to tell you *why* we decided to live a humbler life. It wasn't because we didn't have the money. We simply wanted to show you and your sisters you didn't need a lot of money to be happy. We should have sat you all down when you were old enough to know the difference and explain."

"You didn't have to," Harris said, cutting his dad off just a bit, ready to make an admission of his own. "A part of me knew. But it was easier to use that as an excuse. To tell myself I didn't want to have to limit my family one day. So, I'd work and accumulate now, so they'd never know what it felt like to want. To not have to hear the words, 'no' or 'we can't afford it.'

"By the way," Harris grinned, trying to add a bit of humor, "I knew you were lying when you told me we couldn't afford those Gretzky skates." Harris shook his head at the memory of being so angry with his dad, when really, he'd gotten a brand-new pair of skates only a month earlier at the start of the season.

Charles chuckled a bit and rocked his own head back and forth, sharing the memory.

"I'm ashamed to admit," Harris went on, "it took a little Christmas magic to get me to realize all of this."

"I wonder if it isn't so much Christmas magic as a woman who believes in spreading it?" Charles asked and waited for his son's reaction.

Harris thought back to the way Harlow had abruptly cut their last night together off early and walked him out without giving him the truth about why she'd really wanted him to leave. He knew something was wrong, but hadn't pressed. Because it had been easier not to press. When his hands smeared down his face and fell, he huffed.

"I think I've managed to fall in love. But," he added, "I've failed to let her know that."

"Ah, yes." Charles knew all too well the unsaid pangs of love. "How about her family?" Charles asked, "Were you and Brandon able to track them down?"

"It will be a Christmas miracle if they make it," Harris said. The combination of flight delays, connections, holiday travel, and winter weather were proving to be the perfect storm of obstacles hindering his plan.

"You've done all you can," Charles assured, then let silence sit between them as he watched Harris' mind ignore the offering of assurance.

"When will you get out of here today? Your mother sent me out to get you in person. She has a feast waiting at home."

Harris smiled as he thought about the production his mom served up for Christmas Eve dinner. Something that would hold them over until midnight Mass – or so they said. They always seemed to find themselves drifting to the kitchen to fill up on seconds only a few hours later, and again upon their return from church.

"Right now. Let's go home and celebrate Christmas Eve." Harris said, not wanting to waste another minute.

Charles watched Harris walk around his desk and leave his laptop behind as he moved toward the door to gather his jacket.

Delighted his son was finally leaving work behind, he too got up to join Harris at the door. With a fatherly pat on Harris' shoulder, the two men walked out of the office and by all of the empty cubes, knowing they wouldn't return until after they'd let Christmas joy lead them right into the ring-in of the New   Year.

CHAPTER 30

After Mass and their third round of Christmas dinner when they returned home, everybody piled into their childhood bedrooms and fell fast asleep. Harris had watched his family climb the stairs in their new red and green holiday pajamas, using only the glow of the Christmas tree to light the way to their rooms.

He was tired too, but as he sat in front of the tree now, he had a feeling he wouldn't be able to sleep.

Harris glanced at the time on his phone and saw it was already four in the morning, and that he hadn't received a call or a message from Harlow. He would send her a Merry Christmas message in the morning, and hope Santa could deliver on her last wish – he was afraid the best he could offer at this point was hope that her family made it.

Snuggling lower in the chair, Harris let his eyes grow heavy and the twinkling lights blur as the tired exhaustion from the day took him over.

Harris woke to glass bulbs clinking together on the tree. He looked around without seeing anybody – or anything – and watched until the ornaments stilled. Then he noticed a card beneath the tree that had *Harris* written in swirly script writing that hadn't been there the night before.

He grinned, wondering if his mom had tiptoed down to sneak it under the tree while he slept. Quietly, Harris lifted the blanket off of him and slunk down to the floor feeling like he had as a young boy.

He was always the first to wake. He would sneak down to the tree, amazed at the beautifully wrapped gifts that had appeared during the night. And, he admitted, the magic of it all. Because it meant Santa had been there.

The red envelope was sealed with an embossed golden sticker. The raised image was a simple, elegant sleigh.

Harris looked around wondering if he should open the card or wait until the rest of his family was up to join him. That had always been the rule – no gift opening until everybody was up. And usually after mom and dad had brewed, and were sipping on, their first cup of coffee.

Kids, he mused, didn't often understand that after returning from midnight mass, three hours of sleep wasn't quite enough rest.

He smiled, letting the childish impulse take him over and slid his finger under the seal until it popped open and snapped as the sticky glue separated from the paper.

The shiny gold card had the same simple sleigh with raised edges on the front. When he opened it there was no store-bought greeting or poem like he would have found in a mass-market greeting card that sent holiday wishes of love to family and friends. Only the same style of scripted writing that read:

> *Harris,*
>
> *I'm sorry I can't be there in person to send you my holiday greeting, but I've had a long night and there are some last-minute Christmas miracles I need to tend to this morning. I hope you can understand.*
>
> *I want to let you know how very proud I am of you and the selfless man you've become. It seems to make the season a bit more magical, don't you think?*
>
> *I'm hoping I can ask a favor of you, and I feel there's nobody more worthy of the task than you. Somebody who understands the true beauty of the season.*
>
> *I won't get a chance to pick up any last minute Christmas letters that might have found their way to the postbox, so I'm hoping you'll find time to go take a look for me. If you find any, go ahead and open them, and I'm sure you'll know what to do.*
>
> *Merry Christmas, Harris. And have a wonderful New Year.*
>
> *SC*

Harris read the letter three more times, then stared at the signed *SC.*

It couldn't be, he thought, *there's no way.*

But as crazy as it might have been, if there were unanswered letters in the postbox, he had to go.

He'd seen the faces of the kids at Heritage House when he delivered the news and the invitations for the Christmas Party – all of them full of jubilation. If there was the slightest chance he could come through – even if it was last minute – to make somebody's Christmas Day magical, there was no way he couldn't go.

Still dressed from church the night before, Harris threw on his coat and hat, judged the snow that was falling outside through the front window, then found his winter boots.

When he heard footsteps behind him he figured it was Kayla or Ashley, but when he turned and saw his mom's questioning face he smiled.

He moved over to her, offered a kiss and a *Merry Christmas*, and said, "I'll be back for Christmas breakfast." Then he was out the door.

The roads were more slippery than he thought they'd be, and they hadn't cooperated with his desire to get to the Christmas postbox quickly. He was forced to drive slowly and methodically through the city. The holiday music that played on the radio wasn't helping either. The cheerful beat mocked him as he took a turn at five miles an hour.

When Harris parked, he left his SUV running and the lights on to help guide his path to the postbox as it sat like a red beacon in the dark morning.

It was the perfect Christmas morning, he thought, as the stars still shone above him and snow lightly fell around him.

He lifted his feet in a high march as he navigated the snow bank to access the back of the postbox. When he opened the back with a twist of the lever, he grinned as he recalled Harlow attempting to get her own letter out. He had to admit, he hadn't wanted to tell her how to open it, even though he'd already had her letter. There was something about that moment, the cute denial of her mission. It was, he realized, the first time she'd strung a little bit of her own Christmas magic around his heart.

There was one letter sitting in the bottom of the box. Harris reached in, pulled it out. He stared at the envelope and the writing – and let hopefulness and familiarity rush through him. He held it knowingly, but wondering what he would find inside.

He removed his glove and slid a finger under the seal, then unwrapped the folded paper to reveal a picture of himself and Harlow, holding hot chocolates as they shopped for Christmas trees together for the first time.

The spark of love burned through him as he recalled the memory. Seeing the two of them together, one arm innocently around the other, not knowing yet that they would find love. And as he slid the picture aside, there was only a single wish on the list:

10. To fall in love

CHAPTER 31

Harlow woke early but lingered in bed letting the glow of the Christmas tree, and the glow of her cell phone, welcome her to Christmas morning.

For just a moment, when her eyes opened, she expected to feel sadness – but when she looked at the messages from Lisa that had come pouring in over the wonderful Christmas Eve night, not an ounce of sorrow could be found.

Elated tears filled her eyes and she scrolled through laughter, hugs, and more heartfelt exaltation than she'd ever seen, as Lisa, Steve, and baby Layla brought their treasured new son home for Christmas.

They'd captured Mikey's innocent wonder as he walked through the door of his new home. The way he cheered as he walked into a bedroom that was decorated just for him. How he'd clung to and snuggled his new, fluffy teddy bear that he no longer needed to keep him safe, but would cherish for the rest of his life.

Harlow closed her eyes and smiled. So happy, she swore she heard the sound of laughter fill her head.

When the laughter didn't stop, she grinned as she imagined her neighbors must be reuniting with family for the holiday.

At…six in the morning, she saw when she looked at the top of her phone. That's weird, she thought.

The happy sound called to her and drew her out of bed. She couldn't help but want to see the commotion, to be a part of it, even if her role was just as a nosy neighbor.

She pulled her robe over her flannel pajamas, slid on her slippers, and headed down the stairs.

The noise grew louder the closer she got to the door, and she giggled at the thought of people seeing each other after being away. The image of people embracing when Christmas finally allowed them to push all other excuses aside and come home.

Harlow flipped the lock on the door and opened it. When she did, five faces separated from a circle – where they'd been holding each other and laughing – and looked up at her, staring with huge grins.

As Harlow took in their smiles, tears filled her eyes for the second time that morning. She brought her hands to her face and whispered in disbelief, "Mom? Dad?" then paused, unable to get the rest out.

Before Harlow could say any more, shouts of joy in greeting and more laughter bellowed out as her parents, her brother and his wife, and her sister ran up the steps, enveloping her with their arms and bodies, repeating variations of "Merry Christmas, Harlow!" and "We love you!" over and over again.

Harlow couldn't believe the wonder of the moment. She had so many questions, but none of them could escape, because everything inside of her was too busy overflowing with love. When she tried, only half of the words made it. "How did you-?" and "When did you-?"

Vivienne, Harlow's loving mother, leaned back ever so slightly from their embrace. "We got a call from a man asking us to come home for Christmas – whatever the cost. In fact, he offered to pay for it."

Vivienne's hand rested on Harlow's cheek then she did the same to Vincent and Catherine, her brother and sister. "My sweet babies," she started, then looked at Harlow. "I had no idea."

Vivienne's voice trembled, so she stopped, tilted her head then shook it, unable to tell them she and her husband hadn't realized how badly her children wanted to be together as a family for the holidays.

She'd thought they'd all moved on with their own lives. So rather than be home and missing them, she and her husband had traveled. Taking in and experiencing the holidays somewhere new.

"I'm so happy you're all here," Harlow said, pulling them in once more, not wanting to let them go. And, as she held her family, her mind drifted to the man who she'd completely misread.

Harlow thought of the call she'd received from Brandon only nights earlier. He had called to make sure she was here – and she supposed, if she wasn't, to get her here. She remembered the relief he'd had when she told him she was already in St. Paul and she'd be here at The Hill.

She laughed at the miscalculation, but more at the joy and humor of the realization.

Harris had done this. Her family was the *business that couldn't wait*. What a wonderful realization.

"Let's get inside," Walter Hill said after giving them all another squeeze. "We can catch up over a Christmas breakfast. Harlow," he added," I hope you have food – it was a long flight!"

Enough to feed a small village, she thought, picturing all of the left-over food from the Christmas party. Then she waited and watched in disbelief as her family walked into the house before her.

Everything was perfect. The only thing that was missing was Harris, because more than anything she wished he could be there to see what a beautiful and amazing thing he'd done.

Then she heard his voice.

"Harlow! Harlow!"

She turned toward the sound and heard the footsteps from her family pause in the doorway and turn with her.

As she looked out she saw Harris running, sliding, and skidding down the snow-covered sidewalk, waving his arms toward her, and even more fervently when he saw her look his way.

"Harris?" she asked, more to herself out of confusion, knowing he wouldn't have heard her.

Harlow stood wide-eyed as she let the disbelief fade away. Then she took the stairs to the driveway slowly wondering how in the world he was there, just when she'd never wanted him more.

Her smile turned into laughter as she watched him grin like a child as he ran, laughing at his unsteady feet in the snow, but not wanting to slow his movement toward her. As he grew nearer and slowed his pace, she started jogging in his direction.

Both wanting nothing more than to be in each other's arms. As the gap between them closed, they launched into an embrace that sent them spinning, and holding each other tightly.

As their turn came to a stop, they held each other at arm's length. Harlow's hands came to Harris' face, unable to find the words of affection that could do justice to the miracle he'd given her. *He* was her Christmas wish.

"I found this," Harris said, leaning back and holding up her Christmas letter and the innocent picture of the two of them, not yet knowing they were going to fall in love. "I figured there was still time to make sure you got everything you wished for this year."

Harlow shook her head as her eyes filled.

"I love you, Harlow Hill. You have filled my heart with joy and enchanted my life. Merry Christmas."

Harlow brought herself closer to him and wound her arms around his neck.

"I love you, Harris Porter. So very much. Merry Christmas."

After Harris made a checked-off motion with the letter and let it fly in the air, he brought his arms around Harlow, leaned in, and shared the perfect Christmas kiss with the woman he loved.

Both of them were so overwhelmed with the magic of love on Christmas, they didn't even notice the cheers coming from the steps behind them – they simply fell into the magic and wonder of a simple letter: postmarked, Christmas.

THANK YOU!

I'm so humbled that you've taken the time to read my book. I can't tell you how much of my heart goes into each and every word.

I WOULD BE SO GRATEFUL FOR YOUR HONEST REVIEW OF:
Postmark Christmas

Click the link, or scan the QR code below to be taken to Amazon.
(Hover your phone over the image!)

CLICK TO REIVEW

LOOKING FOR MORE?

Take a look at this seasons' latest releases!

Then, step into the hilarious world of the *Taking Chances* series! Read a special excerpt from **Becoming Us**, then subscribe to Katie's list to read it for free.

NEW RELEASE

THE PROBLEM WITH LOVE POTIONS

The Problem with Love Potions is the sweet, happy, and hilarious fall rom com you've been looking for. Alice is just an average witch trying to get her soulmate to fall in love with her. She didn't try to give her love potion to *everybody* in Lantern Lane…but she did.

Click the link, or scan below get your copy.
(Hover your phone over the image!)

GET THE PROBLEM WITH LOVE POTIONS

COMING SOON

K A T I E
BACHAND

A BORROWED CHRISTMAS LOVE STORY

A Borrowed Christmas Love Story is a sweet, Hallmark-style holiday romance that thrusts two people into the unknown love stories of their grandparents. Perhaps both were too quick to judge their grandparents' decision to remarry so late in life. And perhaps the love story they learn about isn't unlike their own.

Click the link, or scan below get your copy.
(Hover your phone over the image!)

GET A BORROWED CHRISTMAS STORY

COMING SOON

THE WORST CHRISTMAS WIFE

The Worst Christmas Wife is a laugh-out-lough, holiday rom com about one (extremely handsome) grumpy boss that needs a wife, one over-qualified new assistant that needs a raise and a promotion, and two attracted-to-each-other people who hate that they need each other to make it happen.

Click the link, or scan below get your copy.
(Hover your phone over the image!)

GET THE WORST CHRISTMAS WIFE!

FAVORITE HOLIDAY ROMANCES

KATIE
BACHAND

WAITING ON CHRISTMAS

Waiting on Christmas is Katie Bachand's best-selling holiday romance. Fall in love this holiday season on a magical Christmas Tree Farm with two people who were destined to be together.

Click the link, or scan below get your copy.
(Hover your phone over the image!)

GET WAITING ON CHRISTMAS!

AN EXCLUSIVE EXCERPT

A TAKING CHANCES PREQUEL

BECOMING US

A Coming of Age Rom Com

KATIE BACHAND

CHAPTER 1

At about the same time that Grace was applying her baby-pink lip gloss in her apartment mirror, Rachel was sitting in her kitchenette sipping the last of her morning tea and trying to steal one last page of her latest romance novel before making her way out the door. Casey was across town trying to slide her naked body out from beneath a lanky, jet-black-haired man. Unfortunately, the sticky sweat from their morning romp was starting to dry, making the sheets and the misleadingly heavy man nearly impossible to slide out from beneath.

Did this guy die or pass out almost immediately?

Casey filtered through her years of schooling and determined he most likely passed out from the melatonin that graciously accompanied the prolactin, vasopressin, and oxytocin that rushed throughout his body during the last orgasm. Nothing like a good old natural sleep aid to assist with her morning escape.

Giving the sheet one final rip from where it was trapped below the curve of her butt, it came free, and with it her entire body. She hit the floor with a self-conscious, heavy thud. She quickly covered her mouth to mask the grunt that escaped with the landing and slowly lifted her head to peek her eyes over the top of the bed.

Still sound asleep. Fascinating.

Crawling across the floor to her boy-short undies, she slid them on and mentally defended her choice in undergarment as she tried to hop her butt off the floor for the final tug. When that didn't work, she laid down and lifted her pelvis to the ceiling like Grace had made her do when she was on a workout kick.

Mumbling, "Wear the thong! You'll be happy you did when he convinces you to go home with him." Casey smiled as she thought of the chance to flaunt her big-underwear victory. "Looks like I don't need fancy undies after all."

Rolling across the floor to her tapered dress pants she wore to the business dinner the night before, Casey dragged them over her legs with her feet pointed skyward.

With all this exercise she wouldn't even feel bad declining Grace and Rachel's invite for a run after their meeting today.

After wriggling into her matching jacket, she laid on the floor with her arms and legs wide, and gave a crackling yawn. God, she was tired. She didn't drink much as a general rule, but had pulled the all-nighter with the big boys before half-heartedly agreeing to go home with the youngest member of the financial planning team. He was cute, but one look at him looking at her, and she knew he was all wrong. He had that long term look in his eyes. One she was trying to avoid staring into this morning.

Instead, she'd stare into the eyes of her two best friends over a giant cup of coffee. She'd give them hell about getting her up too early, hear whatever it was Grace was so eager to tell them, then slink off to her apartment for sweats and a long morning nap. Then, maybe she could convince them to meet her for an early dinner.

Casey's grin scowled as she reached blindly for the doorknob. On all fours, inches away from freedom, she thought it wasn't such a bad start to the day.

It was Spring, and the sun was finally bouncing light between the buildings on the city's east side. It was a brisk sixty, but Grace loved the chill and knowing that as soon as the sun reached her, she would warm.

Everything about the way she was feeling lent to the long, confident stride. Grace felt how she imagined she would in the countless daydreams of becoming a successful businesswoman. Everything from the Master's Degree, to the office cubicle, to the professional attire she'd get to flaunt.

In a few short weeks, she would ride up the elevator to Thomas and Jane, LLC with her dad for the first time as an employee. She'd no longer be just visiting, or stopping in for lunch, or be the intern.

But first, she had another little business venture she wanted to tackle. If Thomas and Jane was going to be her new home, she wanted to spruce the place up a bit. And that included the dilapidated old building that sat just in front of the old paper mill that held their offices.

Grace picked up the pace, only blocks away from her building, smiled at the tray of coffees she was carrying for her friends, and let herself get excited about what was to come. She couldn't wait to share the news with Casey and Rachel.

Driving the five miles into the city to meet her friends, Rachel's hand pressed against her heart as she thought about the terrible misunderstanding her hero and heroine just had in the latest romance novel she was devouring. It took all of her strength to place it on her kitchenette table and walk away.

"It's just so, so, heartbreaking," Rachel said to herself as she felt compassion rip at the edges of her chest.

When she turned down the street that would take her to Thomas and Jane, Rachel had to shake off the sadness starting to consume her. Why did these books always do this to her?

The voice in the back of her mind told her she knew why. But her mind blocked out that annoying little nag, and she shimmied her body and made a lip-ruffling sound to go with it to shake it off.

As she crept closer, she no longer had to change her tune. When she saw Grace approaching Casey with a pile of coffees in hand, Rachel squealed with delight. She loved her friends, and there was nothing in the world she would rather be doing early on a Saturday morning.

"There are eight million things I'd rather be doing right now than staring at this pile of sticks and bricks. A nap is one of them." Casey swung for the coffee Grace held out for her and scowled at how put-together her blonde friend was at seven in the morning.

Grace didn't try to hide the once-over she gave Casey, evaluating the formal business attire, smudged makeup, and matted hair.

"Oooh, coffee!"

Grace turned toward the enthusiastic sound and offered Rachel the first cup.

"Thanks!" Rachel grinned out the words as she looked at Casey. "You are *the worst* morning person. Are you wearing – oh my God." Rachel inched closer, their noses nearly touching. "You look...glow-y. Shiny. And exhausted!"

"I don't look anything. And 'glow-y' isn't a word."

Ignoring her irritable friend, Rachel turned her nutmeg eyes to Grace as she asked, "You see it? Tell me you see it."

Grace couldn't believe she hadn't caught it. Messy, yes. Unkempt – absolutely. The laziest morning person in the world – nailed it. But she hadn't seen it. Leave it to the Love Guru, Rachel, to pick it out at first glance. She had been so caught up, excited for the surprise, that it slipped right by.

"Oh," Grace admitted after further examination, "I see it."

"Who is he?" Rachel's tone dropped an octave, all business.

"Stop." Casey sipped her admittedly delicious coffee and motioned to the street corner. "Okay, we're here. Tell us why in the hell we're here." Wishing more than ever she'd at least thought to bring sweats. It would have made the disheveled look a little more believable.

"No way. Not until you give us a name." Grace stood by Rachel's side, a barricade to information. They knew Casey would be too curious to leave. She'd cough up the details.

Casey's head fell back with an exaggerated sigh. "I know what you're doing."

"Whatever do you mean?" Rachel asked, plastering a smile on her face, then casually crossing her arms and letting her coffee nonchalantly rest on the edge of the fold.

"You know why I look the way I do. But I'm not interested in explaining the scientific impacts of sexual intercourse on the human body just because you think I'm *glow-y*. You also know that I want to know why we are here. So you're flaunting what you've yet to explain."

Grace spoke out of the side of her mouth to Rachel. "She's right. We're flaunting."

"Absolutely." Rachel nodded.

"I hate you."

"Oh, now that's not nice. We just want to know who he is."

Playing along, Rachel looked at Grace. "She's kind of cute when she acts so smart."

"And grumpy."

"Yes," Rachel nodded in agreement, "and grumpy. A cute, grumpy."

"I am smart." Casey huffed and took another swig, burning the back of her tongue. She swallowed and shook her head. "Lane Kohl."

"And?" Rachel pressed.

"And he's a financial manager that I met with to talk about investments. Decent in bed. I'll never see him again."

"Hold on. You have money?" Grace asked. "We just graduated."

"Hold on. Why just *decent?* And why are you never going to see him again?" Rachel followed up.

Casey had to actively stop her lips from turning up. Because just like that, her two friends defined themselves in their questions. Grace, all business; Rachel, all love.

"Yes," Casey looked at Grace, "I found investors who are interested in the dating app I just finished."

Then she turned to Rachel. "Yes. No sparks – because those don't exist. And confirmed, I'm never going to see him again."

"Why?" Grace and Rachel asked in unison.

"Because he called me this morning after I snuck out asking when he could see me again. Now," Casey moved on, knowing they wouldn't press any further about why she refused to settle down, "tell us why we're here."

Rachel gave a slight nod, agreeing to give up on the interrogation – for now.

Grace smiled and said, "We're going on a vacation."

"We are?" Rachel screamed, all excitement. "I don't have any money. But I'm never going to have any money. So, let's go!"

"Where are we going?" Casey asked, grinning at Rachel, Minnesota's newest broke grade school teacher.

"France."

"Oh," Rachel's dreamy voice purred, "we are *really* going on a vacation."

"Yes, we are." Grace took in a deep breath, still having a good feeling about everything, and eyed the run-down brick building that sat beneath Thomas and Jane, LLC, her dad's accounting firm. The firm she would soon be working for – right after a quick vacation.

The building might have been a crumbling add-on to the old paper mill her future office sat in. But she had a mind for business, and with her father's blessing, she was taking on a little venture of her own before she parked herself upstairs.

KEEP READING BECOMING US

For a limited time, get ***Becoming Us*** FREE when you sign up for Katie Bachand's Newsletter!

Click the link, or scan below get your FREE copy.
(Hover your phone over the image!)

GET BECOMING US

BOOKS BY KATIE BACHAND

SERIES

Taking Chances Series:
Becoming Us (Prequel)
Conflict of Interest (#1)
In the Business of Love (#2)
A Business Affair (#3)
Betting on Us (#4)

STANDALONES

Romantic Comedy:
The Problem with Love Potions

Christmas Novels:
Postmark Christmas
Waiting on Christmas
A Borrowed Christmas Love Story
The Worst Christmas Wife

ABOUT THE AUTHOR

KATIE BACHAND is the author of contemporary romance, sweet romantic comedy, wholesome holiday romance novels.

KATIE lives with her husband, sons, and golden retriever in beautiful Minneapolis, Minnesota. She hopes in her novels, and in life, you find great friendships, great love, and great appreciation for our wonderful world and the people in it.

Visit Katie on her website at
https://www.katiebachandauthor.com

Or, find Katie on any of your favorite social media outlets by following the link below, or searching **KATIE BACHAND** on Facebook and Instagram.

https://www.instagram.com/katiebachandauthor

https://www.facebook.com/katiebachandauthor